BUII

UNIVER

Max Murgia

Elwin Croxsford and the Land of Shardana

Max Murgia

europe books

www.europebooks.co.uk | info@europebooks.co.uk

ISBN 9791256972593
First edition: March 2026

Elwin Croxsford
and the
Land of Shardana

“Elwin never imagined that his daily morning walks would change his and his friends life forever”

Dedicated to my wonderful parents, especially to my mother that has always encouraged me to achieve my full potential.

After finishing this manuscript, my first of three, possibly more to come, book, a book that took me into a fantastical world that would never have been possible in reality; my imagination knows no bounds, and this first piece of writing is a proof of that.

I thank myself first and foremost, with sheer willpower I was able to realise my dream, hoping it will become an infinite dream, so much so that I feel at one with the very story I created and millions more will dream with me.

Also, I want to thank my Parents for their patience and helping me in finding the Sardinian names of the places that are mentioned in this book with much laughter, especially for them to remember when they were young and spent time there with their parents.

To my editor Veronica Parise for her patience on editing my first book and all the others involved on the creation at Europe Books.

Also, most of all, I want to thank the Divine Goddess, because without her, giving me the time and privilege, I wouldn't be able to create the Shardana's magical world.

Preface

In this first book, I wanted to create a fantastical story, about the struggle of the daily life of a typical bunch of teenagers, that, I may say, could be some snippets of my teenager's years growing up in the 1980 in Sardinia.

To empower and give them a reason to love and accept themselves for who they're and the beautiful human interaction between them, and not only in view of all the very dangerous tasks that, they need to face during their stay in the magical world of Shardana, a fantastic place that will test their courage and loyalty to each other and to all the other incredible creature that will cross their lives in this amazing adventure, but also the amazing experiences with all the good inhabitants too, that they're willing to help on the quest. You may say, "why are they taking this dangerous route?". "For what purpose?".

One of thc reasons could be that these teenagers, with their struggle in their daily lives, together, involuntary, summoned an 'Angel', in the form of Adriana, that at the same time saw the goodness in their hearts, in the form of the 'Iag Energy', that is a powerful weapon against the forces of darkness, although they have no idea about the powers that they possess and that's why Adriana and some other key creatures from the land of Shardana, comes to the rescue on helping to develop it and giving them, at the same time, courage, strength and honour, transporting you too, to this fantastic tale.

The second could be that there isn't any reason at all and this situation, may that be, only a dream that are experiencing together on the night in the park, because of their very vivid imagination, a daily way, on to cope in their lives.

The third and finally one, is for you to decide, the reader to get transported in the magical land of Shardana, experiencing all the highs and lows in the company of the group during their quest and looking forward to the next chapter in the second book.

The events and characters depicted in this book are fictitious. Any similarity to actual persons, living or dead, is purely coincidental.

Chapter One

'The unusual morning walk'

The landscape was dark and bleak, the sky ominous and with a heavy atmosphere. All of a sudden, the ground beneath him, was shaking violently.

Cracks started to appear, emanating blue flames.

All around shadows of different shapes and sizes, came nearer him, trying to grab his legs and arms, that all of a sudden, a bright light, came down from above, almost next to him, with three silhouettes made of pure light.

Opening his eyes. "What was that?" Elwin said with his hearth racing; "Was only a dream!".

A very vivid dream indeed.

After some breakfast, he made his way out to go to school.

Looking at the mountains in front of him, thoughtfully he stopped and wondered about his day.

Elwin was a relatively quiet, a bit shy for a teenager and of an unusual looking boy, about fifteen years of age. For no apparent reason to him, lots of people found that he had a unique and different look.

Was it, how he looked? Very pale, bright green eyes and almost white hair.

Maybe was because they're jealous, although being shy of his outgoing and free-spirited attitude.

He definitely didn't care about it.

Was a lovely January morning, cold but sunny, he was walking on his way to school, cutting through his local park, a lovely dog, to be precise a labradoodle, honey coloured like an appealing scone with clotted cream on top, approached him and stopped, looking straight at him in the eyes with curiosity; he looked back at the dog and in his mind, this dog, introduced himself to the boy. “Hi, my name is Okie!”, “What’s yours?”.

With a flabbergasted face, the boy answered back to him; “mmm…my name is Elwin!”. He was so surprised that the dog could communicate to him telepathically and was very friendly too, also he was happy by this very nice and polite boy, usually his owner, was not so very nice to him, so it assumed that most of the humans were like him; “Okie?”, Elwin asked, “Would you like to become friends?”. Okie replied, that he was more than happy to become his friend.

In the distance, Elwin could hear a very rude and unpleasant voice. A man was calling Okie.

An unattractive big man, with lots of personal problems and he took his frustration on the dog or anyone in which had the misfortune to cross his path. With a nod, they said goodbye, wishing each other a good day, and Okie hinting, that they would meet up again, very soon. Elwin with a perplexed face, proceeded back on his way to school.

Further down the path, a squirrel moved swiftly in front of him. Stopping and looking at Elwin; he looked at the squirrel back in the eyes. The squirrel greeted him and introduced himself; “my name is Baku!”; Elwin with reluctance, replied; “I’m Elwin!”, nice to meet you Baku!”, Baku also asked; “Would you like to be my friend Elwin?”, Elwin, again very surprised, agreed.

Then Baku said: “I hope to see you tomorrow, Elwin!” Not paying much attention to what Baku just said to him; he agreed with a nod. Continuing on his way to school, next to a beautifully manicured pond, Elwin noticed, a voluptuous white goose. “Good morning, how are you today?”, the goose asked him. Elwin, again in shock, looked at the goose and realising, that she could understand and talk to him too, replied, “I’m very well, thank you very much!” and this time, Elwin introduced himself to her first.

“My name is Elwin and is very nice to meet you!”. “What’s yours”; “mine is Madame Bijoux!”. Madame Bijoux with an, almost aristocratic manner, bowed her head.

Elwin wasn’t sure on how to react as he did with the others, but he tried anyway. “Can we become friends, Madame?”, he asked; “Of course, we can be friends, Elwin, I was about to ask you anyway!”. “I’m in here often in this pond with my family and friends!” hinting to the other geese further down the pond and a mixed lot of different water birds.

“So, when you are passing through, just call me and I will come to see you and we can have a lovely chat!”.

“Oh yes, we need to talk very soon!”. Elwin a bit confused by that assumption, but with a very positive feeling, greeted Madame Bijoux goodbye and again, he continued on his way to school.

Further down the park a robin perched on top of a fence, looked at him, Elwin stopped. “Good day!” “How are you doing today?”, the robin asked him.

Elwin not anymore surprised by this situation, replied “very well!”; “How do you do?”, “my name is Elwin, and I’m very well, thank you!”. “What’s yours?”. “My name is Scarlet!”.

Elwin with a very pleased face, replied to Scarlet, that in response asked him if they could be friends; “I would love to!”, Elwin replied: “I’m always in here and about, so when you are passing throughout the park, feel free to call me, I would love to have some company!".

"A very special company indeed!", Scarlet replied, "Thank you Elwin!", we definitely need to meet up very soon!" A bit surprised by that answer that was similar to the one of Madame Bijoux.

Elwin, was more and more surprised and perplexed by what was going on that morning, meeting all this very 'unusual friends', he thought. With the cold wind and the sun on his face, he continued on his way to school, with no worries in the world, whatsoever.

Further down the path, a beautiful, shinning black crow, perched on a low branch, looking at him and with an almost regal posture, realising, that was true what the others were saying, that this boy could understand and talk to them, at least mentally, he asked Elwin where he was going, Elwin, surprised that this crow already knew is name, explained to it, that he was on his way to school and asking what was his name. "My name is Richard!", the crow replied; "What a regal name you have Richard, and he's a pleasure to meet you, sir!", "would you like to be friends Richard?", with reluctance, the crow paused for a second and finally agreeing and saying to him. "Well, I suppose we could be friends!", "I always detested humans, but I think, that you are a very special one as they said, and I think that we shall meet again, soon!".

"I like you Elwin!". Richard continued. "Thank you very much Richard, I do like you to, may I ask you, what do you mean when you said, them?"," Who's them?"

Without answering his question, "I have to go now, I hope to see you soon!", with a nod of approval, Richard flew away.

Again, Elwin happier and shocked than ever, and he couldn't believe that all of this was possible, it must be a continuation of last night dream or I must be losing my marbles, he asked to himself; after a brief pause, he was pacing faster on his way to school, realising that he might be running late, that out of the blue, a magpie stopped him on his tracks. "Why are you going so fast?", the magpie asked him, in a patronising, demanding and arrogant way. "I'm going to school. How are you today?", Elwin asked her.

That with an attitude of superiority like being annoyed by his assumption, she flew away, without answering his question.

Elwin, without taking any notice of it, stopped to look at his watch and seeing, that he was really running late, speed it up is pace, when a stunningly majestic black cat stood on his way.

"Where do you think you're going?", the cat asked him. Elwin with a not so surprised face anymore - after all what has happened in the last half-hour - replied, "I'm going to school and I can't talk to you at the moment, sorry because I'm already running late and probably I will get in trouble for it!".

"Not so fast my friend, let me introduce myself. My name is Adriana, and I would like to offer you a different and unique way of learning!", confused by this assumption, he tried to understand what this very confident and beautiful cat meant, then Adriana, almost immediately, replied, that she already knew, who he was and explained that, she was looking for a special human to do a very special task, she asked Elwin, to think carefully, why could he understand all of those creatures that he meet earlier, including herself.

Elwin perplexed, bowed his head and reflected upon her question. His mind was spinning.

"She's right! How could all of this situation be possible? I know that, I love all nature creatures, big and small!". Adriana, at the same time was reading in his mind, and what he was thinking and stopped him daydreaming, so she explained in simple words that there was another realm, parallel to this one, that was in danger, and that they needed a human with a pure hearth and an unconditional love for all creatures.

Still Elwin, very confused and a bit scared, but at the same time very curious and intrigued to know more.

Adriana, explained that they needed to meet up tomorrow at about 5pm in this very park, at the foot of the Great Oak at the end of the Old Wall,"Know this dear Elwin, you will need four more companions, pure of hearth, like yourself, for you to be able to get to our realm to help us on the quest; I can't choose them for you, you need to do it yourself, so you need to be very careful, who you choose!" She said: "It was really nice to meet you, now Elwin, be on your way to school and I hope to see you, all of you, tomorrow by the Great Oak. We need you!", she added.

So how quickly the cat appeared, it disappeared as quickly.

Elwin, confused and excited, questioned himself, into thinking what's just happened.

Was all in his mind? Was an imagination, a vision? Continuing walking, faster on his way to school, hoping not to be stopped by any another creature.

He only noticed, Richard the crow and further down, the magpie with no name, were watching him and that made him a bit uneasy. Finally, he arrived at school.

The day was, as always not very enjoyable for him, surrounded with mostly annoying and boring peers and pompous teachers; there was, although few students that had some interesting looks and points of view with similar taste, like himself.

Strange looking, extrovert and generally eccentrics, for society's standards, but they could be 'those friends', yes, those friends that he needed for Adriana's quest, he just needed the courage to ask them.

Chapter Two

‘Recruiting his companions’

Opening the door of his house, back from school and saying a quick hello to his Mum.

Running up the stairs into his room. Dropping the bag on the floor, the room was quite big and light, full of the most amazing ‘artefacts’ that he found and collected in the woods and around the countryside, may that be a beautifully shaped stone, carved slowly by Nature.

May that be a small log that resembles a dragon or a fairy. Anything that had a magical and unique appeal, was highly priced by Elwin. Yes, that word ‘magical’ was very important to Elwin, it was a way to escape the, sometimes, cruel reality of everyday life.

His mum just called him to get down for dinner. She was a lovely lady, Mrs Croxsford, plump and with beautiful bright blue eyes and a kind smile, always there for him and never complaining of his fancy and eccentric antics.

His father the same, was a big and nice man, not much at home, because always at work, but nevertheless, he loved Elwin for how he was, Joseph was is name, but everyone called him, affectionally Ned.

Elwin also has two sisters, Lucretia and Hersilia, a bit younger than him, but generally they did get on, despite being siblings.

Dinner went and as the rest of the family, watched some TV or sitting around the fire place, looking at the crackling flames with Mrs Croxsford, as usual telling fantastical stories to her precious family.

A bit later, Elwin went back to his room and reflected on the situation that happened in the morning. Still, he could't believe it and he couldn't talk about it, with no one.

Who would believe him. They would think he was crazy or something else.

He laid on his bed looking at the celling, thinking, until his eyes, tired of starring to nothingness, wouldn't keep up with the stress of the day, closing them and falling into the arms of the night.

His dreams where strangely relaxed.

He dreamed of all those animals that he saw and meet the morning before, but, they were in a sort of human form, in a strange world but beautifully appealing to him, they were all around him on a circle of Stones with their hands up, creating some sort of dome of pure and bright light.

Morning was finally here. His eyes just opened, he didn't need anyone to wake him up, was always ready for another day, a new day. Still in bed for a few minutes, looking at the window, he could see the mountains. His beloved mountains, with an early mist and snow at the top of the tallest peaks.

He loved to look at them. The village's name Borghmorloch, was a quiet and pretty place and was surrounded by all of those mountains, in all their glory.

He made his way down to the kitchen and his mother was already making breakfast, greeting him good morning with a kiss, she gave him a large cup of warm milk, with some homemade almond biscuits.

She seated on the table with him, while peeling some potatoes, asking how did he spend the night, he wanted to tell her the dream and the encounters from the day before, but he couldn't, even thought that his beloved mother could, actually understand him. He didn't want to worry her, he could't say anything at all.

His two sisters, by now had join them for breakfast.

Again, on his way to school, aware of his surroundings, decided to go and see his grandmother before passing through the park.

That very wise woman that he always loved. Her house was very old and full of vcry interesting antiques and lots of animals; from chickens to pigs, from cats to pigeons, almost a small farm.

Knocking at the door and letting himself inside, she greeted him with a very beautiful smile as always and asking if I had eaten.

"I'm fine Grandma, thanks!". We seated down next to the fire place, and I asked if grandpa and uncle where ok. "They're already out for work in the countryside!" she said.

Looking at the flames in the fireplace, dancing as if they wanted to tell us something, my Grandma, Mrs Potwell, she asked, if there was something troubling me.

As usual she knew that something was not quite right. So, I did explain about what had happened the other day.

She didn't seem surprised at all, after all, you're old in off to understand what I'm about to say.

She confided in me that she could talk to animals too and also my mother was able to do the same.

"You see Elwin, we're descendant from a very long line of what people call, witches!". She explained that not all witches where bad, as unfortunately many people wanted to believe, but actually, most of them were good and always helping all living things, may that be people, animals or the plant kingdom.

Gob smacked and very happy by this amazing discovery and understanding his feelings for Nature; I asked what should I do about Adriana.

With a smile on her face, she told me that I should follow my hearth and feelings.

“You’all know, what to do when the time comes!”. She then stands up and tells me to wait, “I’m getting something for you!”. “What is it?”, Elwin asked. “Is an amulet for protection!”, she said. There it was, handing this bundle to him; five, intricately bounded, small bunch of wheat, with a green string forming a never-ending number eight.

“Keep it, always with you and it will protect your body and soul, when you need it the most!”.

I thanked her with a kiss and went on my way to school.

Passing through the park, he could’t see any of the creatures that he saw the other day. “Very strange!”, he mumbled to himself; there was only those three boys that were always taking the mic of him, so without looking at them, he speeds up, to get away from them.

The day went as usual and he could’t wait to finish it, he made his mind up. “I will meet Adriana this evening and see what I can do to help them or at least to know, why do they need our help! Just remembered what she told me!”, mumbling to himself.

“I need to get four companions!”. “Who could they be, and how can I explain to them this unbelievable story!”.

“I have too!”.

On the lunch break, although being a very cold day, most of the students were outside playing and he saw one of his friends, Aqua, sitting on a bench, alone in the corner.

“Hi!”. “Can I sit next to you, Aqua?”. “Sure!”. Aqua was a very pretty girl, with not only an unusual name, but a look that resemble more of a fairy or an elf.

With stunningly long red hair and beautiful hazel-coloured eyes.

She was always drawing on her little pad note.

Drawings about nature folks and magical creatures so, she seemed perfect as one of the five that he needed it, and hopefully, she would be able to understand his proposition.

We talked about stuff, and I asked if she could join me around the Great Oak on the park this evening for a magical sitting down to look at the full moon.

Yes, that evening was the eve of a beautiful Ice Moon; with a pause, putting down her pencil and looking at me with a pretty smile. “Yes, I will join you!”, she agreed without even thinking twice, hoping to sneak from her house, unnoticed. While they were still talking, two more kids join them, Oscar and Lunette, asking them what they were doing.

Oscar, a stocky, big young man, with a golden hearth and a bit quiet, light-coloured hair and blue eyes.

Elwin always liked him, and he had the same impression that he fancied him as well, but he was too shy to ask; on the contrary, Lunette with her beautiful dark features, almost looking like an ancient Egyptian princess, long black hair and big dark eyes always painted with a black kohl.

Elwin could’t believe his luck, that all those kids that he always liked and admired, are there in front of him and the potential companions that he needed it for the quest. Before he could ask them, Aqua, out of the blue, suggested Elwin to invite them too, for this evening Full Moon’s watch.

His face could't hide his excitement and getting a bit red on the face, with a nod of consent agreed to let them join, if they like it (trying to hide Aqua's perfect timing).

Oscar and Lunette smiled and asked Elwin where they supposed to go. So, after explaining where to meet, they went back inside, Elwin and Aqua shortly followed them.

By now was getting very cold, and the bells ringed to let them know that the break time was finished, but before they managed to get inside, the bullies that Elwin always tried to stay away from, approached the duo and started making fun of them.

They were about two years older than them, the leader's name was Tack, the other two, always behind him, as I called them, Tack's shadows, were Norman and Tristan.

In truth these three guys were actually a very sad bunch, not the brightest of the kids and always picking up on the younger and defenceless students.

Trying their best to ignore them, and being saved by one of the teachers, Mr Othen on the door, in which he gave them a look so fierce, that they left in a rush like cowards, as they're and always will be.

Elwin, in the classroom was thinking that he needed another companion to complete the group of five. On his right-hand side, there she was, another potential 'candidate'.

Alyssa a very pretty girl, that kept herself to herself, very mysterious, always wearing black clothes and extremely pale, shinning blue black, long straight hair, almost ethereal, a proper natural goth, with deep and bright green eyes, like him.

How he didn't think of her before? Definitely very spiritual, but how he would approach her, and explaining what they're up too for that evening?

He was quite shy himself. Then, like she could feel him thinking and looking at her, she turned, looking straight at him; with a gasp and getting red in the face, bowed his head back on his book.

The teacher noticed all of this and with a smile, looked at them through her low small glasses.

That moment brought back memories when she was a teenager herself. Miss Partridge was her name and she was a nice teacher, not like the others, that they were quite strict and absent to the needs of thc teenagers, like Mr Othen.

You could talk to her and she wasn't that old, as the others.

She was around in the mid 30s and quite unusual for a science teacher being that young.

Finally, the day was almost over and Elwin, still had to ask Alyssa to join them for the evening.

Usually, it took him a lightning strike to get out of the classroom, but not today; he remembered that Alyssa was always the last one to go, so he waited and collected his belongings very slowly.

Alyssa noticed that and again she looked back at him with a timid smile and wondering what was going on; that was the signal, he pulls himself together, standing tall, out of his chair towards Alyssa, saying; "would you like to join us this evening for a sit up in the park?".

She was a bit reluctant. "Who's else is going to be there?", she asked.

"Well, myself, Aqua, Lunette and Oscar!", he replied to her. "I'll consider your offer, thanks, but couldn't promise anything!"

A bit disappointed, Elwin smiled at her and saying that he would be very happy if she could make it, promising that would be an evening full of magic and wonders; her eyes sparkled like two shinning emeralds at the word 'Magic' and Elwin, in that moment, knew that she would come to join them.

Chapter Three

'At the foot of the Great Oak'

The time passed quite fast and Elwin could't wait to meet Adriana again and wondering what would be the reaction of his friends.

Would they too be able to speak and understand them? And why Adriana needed five of us!

Why? So many questions to be answered and yet, Elwin's mind wondered higher and higher.

On his way home, passing through the park. Again, no sign of the creatures that he met the other day, he only noticed, that they weren't any people either around and that the atmosphere was different, a bit darker and sinister.

On his left, near some thick undergrowth, he could sense some sort of dark mass, in a not apparent form but alive and pulsating; his senses alerted him to get out of there very quickly; running faster and looking back to see if this 'thing' was following him.

He only noticed that the Magpie without a name was there, staring at him from the branches of a tree. He then questioned himself. "What the heck was that?".

The late afternoon passed very quickly, and with lots of questions and fears in his mind.

Looking out from his bedroom window the sky was very clear, and the moon was surrounded by a bright blue hallow, making it looking beautiful and even more magical.

Almost half four, he waved goodbye to his mum and sisters, telling them that he was going to meet some friends to do some homework together. Mrs Croxsford was very happy to hear that.

He was bonding with his friends and that was reassuring to her, knowing how difficult teenager's life can be. "Be careful?" she said. "Can I come to with you?", Lucretia asked Elwin. "No, sorry Lucretia, another time!", Elwin replied, smiling at her.

He took some food with him, just some apples, a bottle of water and few chocolate bars.

On his way to the park, worrying a bit, about the dark mass that he saw earlier and that some of his friends wouldn't make it for whatever reason.

Aqua has very strict parents, as Lunette, but he hopped that they could make it.

Almost there and the excitement was getting stronger. By the entrance of the park, Oscar and Lunette, were already there, greeting and thanking them; then, Oscar did something that Elwin never expected; he hugged him and his hearth was racing high, getting red faced and embarrassed (but happy at the same time) for what he did in front of Lunette, but she already knew about their feeling toward each other and she was very happy for them. They proceeded towards the Great Oak.

Not many people were in the park at the time; it was a very cold and a bright evening.

They could hear someone shouting at them, that was Aqua, they turn around to meet and hug her, surprised that she could escape so easily from home. Apparently, her father was so drunk, that he collapsed in the sofa early, sleeping it off, also her mum didn't pay much attention either to see if Aqua was in or not. So, off they went towards the Great Oak; only one was missing. Elwin was a bit worried about that.

How Adriana would take it. Also, what about if that was all a dream and she didn't actually exist at all; so many thoughts in his young mind.

At least, if all of this wasn't real, he was looking forward to have some great time with his friends.

Here we were in front of this majestic Oak, that at this time of the year is without leaves, just a splash of green on his trunk, made up by some ivy, that's trying to hung, on the Oak's strong trunk.

Behind the tree was the Old Wall, probably made it long time ago and still standing; full of ferns and moss in between the stones, helping it to stay compact.

It was almost dark and the lack of clouds in the sky and the crisp cold air, was making the moon shining even brighter, lightening the surroundings, even more and making it looking like a surreal and magical place.

Elwin was looking to see if Adriana was around.

Nothing, but somebody else was coming towards them; "Alyssa!" Elwin, rejoiced; everyone was very surprised and happy to see her; she kept her promise. Elwin went towards Alyssa and with a hug, thanked her for coming.

As all of them sat on the foot of the Great Oak, looking at the moon, contemplating and about to ask Elwin, why they were there. Suddenly this majestic black cat appeared in front of them, "Adriana!", said Elwin.

Standing and looking at Elwin, she thanked him for coming. In that moment Elwin knew that everything that had happened the day before, was actually real, and as for magic, Adriana looked at the group, one by one, first was Alyssa, then Lunette, Aqua and Oscar.

All of them could't believe what was happening in front of them.

It was the most amazing and bizarre sensation, so Adriana started to talk to them and introduced herself.

"I'm Adriana, high-witch of the Kingdom of Zinnigha Perdaxa, in the land of Shardana, a parallel world, that's in front of your very eyes, but you have to be a very special person to be able to see it, feel it and enter it!".

Apart for Elwin, the rest of the group was gob-smacked by this talking cat. Alyssa was the first, to ask Adriana, how they could enter or see this magical realm.

"As I explained to Elwin a day earlier, you need to be pure of heart to be able to enter and I know that all of you are pure, that's why we choose you with Elwin's influence!".

The group all turned to look at Elwin in disbelief.

"You're all very kind and have suffered and still suffering today!". She continued.

Looking towards Aqua and Lunette, that both lowered their eyes to the ground. "How could a cat, know my family situation?" Aqua though; "don't be afraid Aqua!", Adriana, said, "You are very special indeed, a beautiful soul and very strong, as all of you are, very special indeed!".

"Now we don't have much time, the Mother Moon, is almost full and we have to enter, between the Great Oak and the Old Wall, but before that, you need to say some words with me, a sort of spell to open the gates and at the same time, protecting all of you, while you are in our world, but remember, that all of you have to say it together at the same time, so when you are ready!" Adriana continued.

Oscar just interrupted Adriana, wondering why they need to go to this fable world. The rest of the group looked at each other, wondering that Oscar had a point and curious of what Adriana would say.

So, Adriana explained, that her world was on the grip of a very evil and powerful witch supported by the Dark One, called Euphenia, arrogant and ambitious, that wanted to overthrow the great King Niuxs VI.

Officially, Euphenia was the cousin of the King, but not in line to the throne, that's belong to the Princess Marygolda, the problem was that the princess was still very young and needs protection; she had lost her mother, Queen Silvarian at birth and although the King loved her very much, Euphenia used a powerful spell, given to her by the Necromancer, which was the right hand on the Dark One to steal the King's mind and to keep him in perpetual darkness and almost in total control. Elwin and the others were gob-smacked by this incredible story.

"The only protection for the Princess Marygolda, is myself and a group of very trusted comrades that live in and around the castle!". Adriana added.

Also, she looked at Elwin, mentioning him that he already had met most of them.

Elwin perplexed, looked at Adriana replying: "your unusual latest morning walk to school?".

Elwin with a smile could't believe that all those 'animals', he had a conversation with yesterday and asked to be his friends, were in fact those fable people and they knew, that they needed his help.

"But how could a bunch of teenagers do something to help?", he asked to himself.

Adriana explained that all of them had a special gift, each of them different but nonetheless, a very important one.

From foresight, telepathy, to be able to talk to all creatures big and small, to communicate with the dead and spiritual beings, to be able to control the elements and the weather.

This time, Lunette asked Adriana. "How would they get away for missing for so long, without making their families worry about their absence?".

Adriana explained that in her world, dimension, space and time were very different and she could make them disappear for a couple of hours in human time, without raising any alarm from their families; but of course, they needed to stay in Zinnigha Perdaxa much longer.

"Don't worry", Adriana assured them, they would be protected. "I can feel that some of you have some personal protection that has been given to you already by your loved ones!", looking toward Elwin; he just opened his bag and amongst the food, was the bundle with the wheat amulet, that his beloved Grandmother gave it to him earlier on that morning. "That's a very powerful protection, you must put it over your neck, close to your chest, so treasure it well!". "I will!", Elwin replied.

Also, Adriana looked toward Alyssa, "you have something very special too! A beautiful star, a pentacle!". Adriana added. Alyssa was a Wiccan and for her not only was a symbol of her faith and protection, but it was being given by a dear aunt of hers that wasn't with them anymore.

"Keep it very close to your hearth and you will always have protection in the moments of need and not only to yourself!"; Adriana said. "I will, I love and miss her so much, my aunt Phoebe!". Alyssa replied.

As for Aqua, Oscar and Lunette, "Do not despair! Here for you!". Adriana gave to each of them a necklace with a crystal as a pendant.

For Aqua, a beautiful white quartz; for Oscar a blue moonstone and for Lunette an Angelite; all of them set in silver. "Now we need to hurry, and I will explain more on the ways. Are you ready to say the chant with me?"

All of them excited, nodded yes, but Elwin perplex asked Adriana, "From where we can read this spell?", “don’t worry Elwin, you will have imprinted on your mind, as soon as I will speak!”.

Adriana begun chanting, in which they, to begin with could’t understand; then as per magic, the words were easily clear to them in their minds.

“As we stand here,

Oh, Great Oak while the Sacred Moon is full

we feel the magic,

we feel the energy,

open this portal,

so, we can enter to this magical realm in protection and light”

Chapter Four

'Welcome to Zinnigha Perdaxa'

As they stand in between the Oak and the Old Wall, a beautiful bright blue light started to envelope the surroundings and the group, taking them in this kind of wormhole, to begin small, then getting larger and larger.

Adriana was in front of them, followed by Elwin, Alyssa, Lunette, Aqua and Oscar.

When they reached the end of this wormhole, they were met by this stunning sight; shores of pure bright greenery and endless forests as the eyes can see. Sticking up in the middle of the forest, a very tall hill, in which a sort of a castle was perched on it, but not a castle as we know in our world, it was made entirely of trees; huge trees and all sort of shrubs and plants, but not cut down as for using in construction materials, but alive as if for magic, where bent and twisted to create this amazing structure, the 'Magic 'of nature.

Adriana, stopped in front of them, then a bright green light, engulfed her.

A stunningly beautiful and tall woman just appeared before them. "Welcome to Zinnigha Perdaxa, I am still Adriana, actually, how Adriana should be!". The group was astounded by this vision. Adriana was a very attractive woman, wearing a long black greenish velvet dress, elegant but simple, smooth long black hair and those eyes were so amazingly bright yellow, they could see you through.

Elwin, being the first one to have meet Adriana, went towards her, to apologise for not believing in her, for all what had happened in those days. "I understand Elwin, it's not easy, please don't worry about it!"; Adriana said.

She had some differences from her human companions. A part those astonishing yellow eyes, she was much taller, and the ears were pointed, as for the feline features, arms and legs were sleek and elongated.

After the first shock, the group sited down for a bit in the ground, still in awe and shock by all this and Adriana, understandably let them rest.

While they were recovering from the shock, this small man came towards Adriana.

He was wearing a light brown jacket, with a red, embroidered waistcoat and a gold chain with supposedly a watch, black tight trousers and black shoes with a very speedy and fast posture.

After greeting Adriana with a courtesy bow, looked at the group and said towards Elwin; "Hi!". Elwin a bit perplexed and very quick to recognise his friend, "Scarlett! Oh my, is that you?". "Yes, dear Elwin!". Welcome to my home world!".

Looking at the rest of the group. "You are, all very welcome!".

Then, went back towards Adriana and gave her a small wooden box, carved beautifully with leaves and flower's motifs.

Adriana opened the box and inside there were some dark purple berries. "This are very special berries, called, sa Mutta!".

Taking one out in her hands; "you need to take one each; they will help you to adjust your bodies to this environment, from tolerating our food, to if you get unwell or injured, heal your bodies very quickly!". She gave each a berry, that they needed it to chew and swallow with some water from Zinnigha Perdaxa sacred well.

They did as told, and that trust that Adriana portrayed, (although just meeting her) was unshakable and she was very proud and pleased by that. Oscar making a funny face drinking the water very quickly because the berry was a bit bitter. They all looked at him with a smile.

Then, Scarlett showed them the way towards the end of the path in which they entered Zinnigha Perdaxa.

The path was luscious green and alive with many little creatures of different sizes and types, buzzing all around, as they were very curious to see these newcomers.

While they were moving and flying around, some of them, emitted some sort of light but from the inside, like bioluminescent, they were glowing and was so beautiful to experience this spectacle, absolutely amazing. Elwin could't keep his joy to himself as the others with their mouths wide open for this sight. "You don't see this spectacle every day, do you! Unfortunately, not in our world", Elwin said.

Then Oscar, said. "Can you imagine, Miss Partridge in here? She probably would make us to do some homework about this world!" Lunette and the others cracked a laugh.

Adriana, looked at them, very happy that they were taking this adventure and task with a joyful mood; they needed it, to be able to finish their task, although being very difficult and dangerous, Adriana had a lot of confidence in the group and starting to see the energy field, glowing around them 'the Iag', but for now let them enjoy this moment.

At the end of the path, a carriage was waiting to take them to the castle; it was made all by living plants and flowers, driven by these six majestic bright white stags with golden saddles, spurs and reins.

Scarlett was at the front of the carriage instead of riding on top of them, because he didn't need to direct them, the stags knew where to go.

When inside the carriage, they realised how spacious it was, again they noticed, that all over the carriage walls, where many more little creatures buzzing around, and that made it so bright and colourful.

Looking from outside the carriage windows, the group where amazed by this beautiful green world. Alyssa, then said to Adriana, "we wished that our world was so green and bright like yours!". Adriana, with a solemn face, answered;

"You are right, Alyssa, unfortunately we are starting to have similar problems as your world. Corrupted individuals, that think only for themselves and their twisted agendas; you see, Euphenia is one of them and probably the most dangerous one here in Zinnigha Perdaxa and they're more dark creatures and entities that live in the underworld and across the Hellebore Forest!". Adriana continued.

"They want to bring this beautiful and peaceful realm into darkness; you know all the mythical creatures that you read in your fantasy books back home? Here in Zinnigha Perdaxa, they're real. Trolls, Goblins, Giants, the Undead and the evil five, a group of dark witches, that want only to create darkness, discord and ill health to the creatures of light!"

Adriana added.

Elwin and the others were listening attentively. "There is also, some that are so dark and ancient, that only few of the elders of this realm have ever seen it; slumbering, unnamed monsters, that live deep in the regions of Riu Marigosu, a labyrinth of gigantic caves and tunnels; yes, you see, that all underneath this world, there is another one, dark and cold, where all this creatures and monsters that I mention, slumber down there during the day, but they come out in the night to roam parts of our forests and cause havoc!". Adriana added.

"We have lived in relative peace, until now, thanks to a powerful enchantment, cast by three of our most powerful elders, that keeps them a bay. They're very old and wise, we call them, 'the Shining Ones' and you shall meet them soon; but a group of corrupted fellow Perdaxiusu (this is what we are called in the bright side of the Shardana realm) want to bring 'back 'the Dark One, so all the creatures of the underworld could roam free in our beautiful realm and destroying it, but we mustn't let them achieve it!".

Then Elwin, asked Adriana, "why did you said, they want to bring back the darkness?".

"Yes, dear Elwin, you see, a very long time ago this world was at war, that raged for thousands of years and I was there, to witness this onslaught.

The creatures of light against the creatures of darkness; many died, and some were captured and enslaved to be used as workers in the tunnels and mines or for food for the Dark One; an evil entity, ancient and old as our Shining Ones, probably even older, that required constant offerings from the creatures of the darkness!" Adriana explained to them.

The group now was starting to look a bit preoccupied by all these dreadful stories, and wondered if they did the right thing to follow Adriana.

Adriana could read their thoughts. "Do not worry, you are not alone. We're here to help all of you, together we are stronger, we need your powerful energy, that is unknown and unexpected to the Dark One!", she added "You speak of our energy, what do you mean Adriana?", Elwin asked her.

"You see Elwin, that you all, as humans and being very young, possess the 'Iag' a kind of energy field which is unknown here in Zinnigha Perdaxa". The group was listening with much interest.

"Our three powerful elders, had foreseen this and entrusted me on the quest to come to your world to meet you Elwin!", Adriana added. "Incredible!" Alyssa said looking at the group.

"The Shining Ones?" Oscar asked. "No Oscar, not them but three of our most important allies, Mobromora, High Priestess of the Dwarves on Monte e'Zinnigha; Styriax, the Wise Mother of the Shadow Fairies and Maxima, the Troll High Priestess of the Guneria Village.

You will meet them soon but not now, you need to meet our King, Niuxs VI, and unfortunately, Euphenia; she will try to stop you, in all the ways is possible!" Adriana said.

"She's got eyes and ears, everywhere in the castle; but, do not worry for now, I do believe that goodness and light will prevail, and understand that a certain degree of darkness is need it for the universal balance of time, and as long the creatures of darkness, will stay away in their caves, we are fine with that. We are all part of the building of the Bright One!"

Aqua, interrupted Adriana, asking. "Who's the Bright One?".

With a serene face, Adriana replied. "It is a pure Being, that created our world and many others, including your one; nobody knows what it looks like or if it exists in a physical form!".

Oscar, then said, “like God?”; “Not like your God, you see Oscar, here we don’t have the need for, what you call in your world, religion; we live in pure harmony and mutual respect, but unfortunately, through the ages, the seed of discord from the dark side, tries to take roots in our peaceful society, and we must uproot those seeds before they germinate, but on the other hand, it might be the same Goddess or God in which humans believe!”.

Adriana added.

“In off talking, wc arc almost at thc castle!”.

Chapter Five

'The day at the Castle'

The carriage stopped in front of this amazingly tall and steep staircase, on which in either side lied hundreds of stunningly ornate large pots with all kinds of flowers and plants.

The group, get off the carriage and proceeded on their way to the staircase with Adriana leading the way.

Lunette went to get a closer look nearer the pots and with amazement, called her friends to come and have a closer look too. Those 'pots' were actually independent small, you can say, villages. Each and every one of them a different one, full of miniature creatures, like very small fairies. Her eyes filled with tears, but they were tears of joy.

Adriana, stopped to tell Lunette and the others; "you see when I speak of harmony and symbiosis with the natural world! But, don't be fooled by their small sizes, believe me, they can defend themselves very well. This is a magical realm, and we all thrive in 'Magic' most of us, fortunately, use 'Magic' for a positive purpose!".

As they were almost at the top of the staircase, they were admiring the breathtaking view of the landscape around them. "Almost there!", Adriana added.

They're now standing before this huge and strong looking door; Adriana, explained to them, that they needed to ask permission to the door, to be able to enter the royal enclosure.

Elwin and the others looked at each other confused and asked what they're supposed to do; Adriana, told them to listen carefully, because she could't say twice, so they needed to memorise the words. "Good morning Douglas, may we enter please?". "That sounds easy to remember!" ; Lunette added. All the group then repeated the words after Adriana.

In the middle of the door, a face materialised. A wise and a bit grumpy old man's face.

"Good Morning to you Adriana, and who are all these young fellows with you?"; Douglas, asked. "They're Knights from the other world for the King's protection, sir!". The group was pleased and with a big grin on the faces for being labelled Knights.

With a bit of an upper lip attitude, "very well, you may enter!", so Douglas then opened the door; the group entered and in either side of this long and wide gallery, there were standing next to each window, this huge guards, to be precise, sixteen of them.

Wearing long, dark red cloaks, but instead of metal weapons, they had in their right hands a long staff, and for each of them, a different one.

Adriana, explained, that they were the personal guards for the castle, called the Ections; an extra protection for the Palace and the upmost loyalty to the regent King or Queen at the time.

While Adriana and the rest of the group, were walking towards the long gallery, this stunning tall man, cloaked in black and very handsome, appeared before them looking towards Elwin. "How are you Elwin?", he said with a deep voice.

Elwin with a smile, recognised on him the crow in his morning walk. "Oh, my Richard, how nice to see you again, in your true form!". Adriana introduced him to the rest of the group, as Richard, the first General of the house of Niuxs, he nodded with a smile, indicating them to proceed; the Ections, then, simultaneously, holding their staffs high with both hands, creating a sort of tunnel were, this beautiful bright white light, emanated from the top of them.

Adriana, explained to the group that this magical light was to make sure that anyone entering the great hall was not a danger to the King and the Royal family.

Elwin then asked, "so, why Euphenia was allowed to enter the Palace, if she was there with an evil intent?". "You are absolutely right, Elwin!", Adriana replied.

"Euphenia is of royal blood, being the King's cousin and for that, the Ections Magic do not work on her and also, she is quite cunning and powerful witch and uses a protection spell for her benefit, but there is a way around it!". The group, carried on walking, engulfed by this amazing white light.

There, at the end of the corridor, in front of them another set of doors, in which these two small fairies, opened with their wands.

Alyssa was so impressed by these little beautiful creatures, they were made off an ethereal bright blue light, almost metallic shine.

Adriana, explained to the group, that those little fairies where Princess Marygolda personal protection; we call them, the Blue Fairies and their names are, Una and Ella.

"They're just checking on all of you out of curiosity!". Adriana said.

With a smile, they thanked them.

The door opened and the group was met by this enormous hall, with in the middle of it, standing very tall, a majestic gigantic walnut tree, and from his wide trunk, spreading all the way the length of the hall, his huge branches.

In the middle and a bit at the bottom of the trunk of this magnificent tree, where two thrones are located, and as everything in this amazing world, they were made by two curved branches, beautifully bent and looking very comfortable.

The top of the hall was so big, that the entire tree was forming a dome, enveloping the entire hall and forming secondary doors and windows; there it was, in the right-hand side of the trunk, the King's throne. He was sitting down, a quite large looking man, wearing purple robes and inlaid by gold treads. His crown was made by flowers and small twigs, carefully and beautifully arranged, in between his two huge horns; yes, like a ram's horns.

Amazed by this sight, they proceed closer to the throne, behind Adriana, that with a courtesy bow, greeted the King.

The King was on the grip of Euphenia's spell, and for that, made his gaze look's like was absent.

He then, lifted his head to look at them, without saying or doing anything. Adriana introduced the group to the King, one by one, first Elwin, Alyssa, Aqua, Lunette and Oscar that at the same moment, this beautiful woman entered, floating down from one of those secondary doors at the top of the room.

Introducing herself to the group; "I'm Euphenia, and may I ask, who are you and why you are here?". Promptly, Adriana interrupted Euphenia and standing in between her and the group, explaining that they were visiting our world, from the human one, to bring some cheer and company to the King and the Princess.

With a very suspicious and nasty look towards Adriana, Euphenia floated towards the throne and mumbled something in the King's ears, which was indescribable to them and the King, again looking at them in a gazed and absent way.

Euphenia, then looked at Elwin in particular in the eyes, that at the same time, he recognised her as the rude Magpie, that she didn't introduce herself to him a day earlier, nevertheless, he was struck by her beauty.

She was wearing a long bright white dress, with some black strikes across the front, beautiful long white hair with a blueish shine, with this stunning light blue eycs and a particular pendant, in silver, with the letters Z and P interwoven and enclosed with a triangle and a circle. The pendant was, the symbol of the coven of the Iroxi, an ancient order, and the letter standing for Zinnigha Perdaxa.

Also, Adriana, was part of the coven of the Iroxi and had a pendant too; a circle within a circle, with some markings, like triangles in different sizes, overlapping each other and also made in silver.

The group by now looked tired and overwhelmed by all this and Adriana noticed that.

A bell rung and two very smartly dressed individuals, entered the great hall. It was a female and a male; the female was quite plump and jolly looking, wearing a long creamy white dress, with a long trail behind it; her mouse-coloured hair, where lifted up by some golden pins, simple but very elegant. The man was wearing a honey-coloured suit, with a golden chain on his waistcoat, also very jolly on the appearance. Both of them looked at Elwin and with a smile, approached him.

"Do you recognise us, Elwin?" "Oh my, Okie and Madame Bijoux, how happy I am to see you again. How are you two? Elwin with a joyful face replied, "we are very well, dear Elwin and very happy that you manage to get to our world and not alone!" Gesturing to the rest of the group with a courteous bow. Okie said.

"In this realm, we are part of the royal household and to make sure that you and your friends, would be comfortable and safe!", Madame Bijoux said and both of them, looking towards Euphenia, that looked very angry and annoyed.

"Lest move on, shall we?", Adriana interrupted, "you are all very tired and need to rest, we shall finish our conversations later on, and you still need to meet our delightful Princess Marygolda!". Adriana said.

"Please Okie and Madame Bijoux, would you mind to show our guests their rooms to get ready for our evening!". Adriana continued.

The group again, bowed to the King, and left the great hall.

With Okie and Madame Bijoux at the front, they were walking in this long corridor; noticing that the walls were made all by moss of different types and small ferns and in between àll this beautiful greenery, was full of all sort of little creatures, some flying around and some picking out from little windows, excited and curious by these newcomers.

Madame Bijoux turned her head to look at them with a caring smile.

Without being patronising, she asked them if they did understand the importance of all creatures in this amazing realm and how important everyone was, in the keeping for the castle, and beyond, didn't matter how small someone was. They nodded in approval.

Elwin, then looked toward all his friends, telling them how fortunate they were to be able to experience all of this beauty. Lunette and Aqua saying that this feels like a dream. "Almost there!", Okie said.

This huge door in front of them just opened; “here we are, the royal kitchens!” Madame Bijoux, said with a comforting smile, almost a motherly one.

The kitchen was a very large room full of all sort of items, pots and pans, plates and food everywhere but all very organize and tidy and with so many, very busy, royal household staff; males and females, with jolly faces, some looking shy by these strangers, some more comfortable by their presence, but nevertheless, all very welcoming.

This little fellow came forward, very confident and upright. He was wearing a reddish, burnt orange, coloured outfit; Okie introduced the head chef of the royal kitchens, but was interrupted by Elwin, that recognised his friend Baku. “How are you?”. I’m very well dear Elwin and is a pleasure to see you again and to be able to cook for you and your friends!”.

The group, then went nosing around in the kitchen.

Madame Bijoux, called them, and took them to another room with a large square table, already prepared with all sorts of delicacies. “Please sit!” Madame Bijoux, said.

Adriana just joined them and seated at the front of the table with all the group around it.

Most of the food was vegetarian and vegan in nature, presented in terracotta plates and wooden bowls, also the cutlery was made in wood. Small fairies then flying with a jug filling up their glasses with the purest and freshest water that they ever seen it and taste it.

Oscar asked Adriana, why everything here was made in wood and terracotta.

Adriana explained that for them, most of the items made in metal or iron were dangerous at the touch and in some cases, it could kill or rend them vulnerable to attack by the dark side creatures; only silver or gold was fine for them to touch and wear, being attributed and blessed by the Moon and the Sun in the Sacred Wells. "In off for now, please eat and enjoy this evening!", Madame Bijoux, ordered them, in a jokingly way.

The food was very pleasant; "some dishes are similar to the one that we have in our world!" Alyssa said. Being a vegan herself, that was a relief. There wasn't any meat of fish on site and that wasn't a relief for Oscar and Aqua, in which meat and fish, was the main staple diet in their families, but nevertheless they had to eat. Elwin and Lunette didn't mind at all, because they weren't so kin on meat or fish anyway. Later on, Adriana noticed that some of them were beginning to look very sleepy and asked Okie to make sure that their rooms where ready and as soon they have finished their dinner to take them to their rooms to rest.

After at about half hour, Adriana stood up and invited them to get to their rooms and gave them her blessing, wishing a good night of sleep.

Elwin then interrupted Adriana, asking if they could meet Princess Marygolda before they went to bed. "You'all meet the Princess tomorrow morning Elwin, for now just have some rest, please!", Adriana replied.

Okie, then took them to an amazing circular big room with five beds; the walls and ceiling, where made all by branches interwoven with moss and ferns and again full of the tiny creatures flying around, making a bioluminescence light, absolutely stunning; each of them got inside their beds and wishing each other goodnight.

Elwin, looking at the ceiling, like when in his own room back home, with the difference that everything here was amazingly real and magical. All of them looking at each other without saying anything, until they could't keep their eyes open anymore.

The night was very bright and serene in the realm of Zinnigha Perdaxa. Adriana, standing outside the door of their room, holding her pendant in her hands, closing her eyes, starting to slowly mumble a protection spell.

Oh Shining Ones,

please, I Adriana, high witch of thc kingdom of Zinnigha Perdaxa,

humbly ask for them to be always protected and looked after,

and to give them the strength and courage for their task ahead,

in light and love".

As she was saying the spell, her persona was washed in a bright green light that, at the same time was enveloping the circumference of Elwin and the group's room.

Pleased, Adriana left.

After about few minutes, from the darkness of the hallway, a figure appears, Euphenia followed by her sly servant, Artier. Very slowly approaching the door, with not so good intention, but thanks to Adriana spell, she could't even touch the door or stay nearby, furious, she left with a screech.

Chapter Six

'The familiars'

The morning lights, passing through the windows, reflected into their faces, they were just opening their eyes and, most of them, realising that in reality this circumstance in which they were experiencing, wasn't a dream at all and they were actually in this fable world. Without saying anything, just looking at each other and smiling, a knock at the door, "may I enter, please!", Madame Bijoux asked, "of course, come in!" Elwin answered, sitting upright on his bed; Madame Bijoux, then with a big smile greeted them good morning and invited them to join her for breakfast.

Lunette, Aqua and Alyssa also asked Madame Bijoux where they could freshen up.

With a smile "please all follow me, you to boys!". Then, she led them into an area with several rooms and each of them choose one. Each room was provided by a natural small waterfall; the water was already comfortably warm for them to wash, also in this world they didn't need any of the likes of shampoos or shower gels to wash; this water was so pure to keep them clean and fresh. The towels were made from the purest cotton that they ever seen and touch it.

As soon they finished washing themselves up, Adriana, greeted them good morning and giving them new clothes to wear." You need to blend with the locals to be more comfortable!", Adriana said and announcing that they would have breakfast with the Princess

Marygolda. “Don’t worry we will keep your old clothes safe for you, for when you have to return home!” adding.

The new clothes were quite simple and comfortable to wear; very similar style for all of them; in cotton and earthy colours, greens, browns and terracotta red/orange tones.

The shoes were more sturdy and very strong, almost like military booths that were very popular in their world too.

The only one that wasn’t very impressed by them, was Alyssa, for she was so in use to wear black all the time and so, Adriana did have the darkest outfit made specially for her.

A beautiful dark green top and trousers which complimented her stunning green eyes.

“I guess, I can live with that!”, she said with a pleased face.

The rest of the group then, also pleased by their outfits, were ready to meet the Princess.

Adriana, leading the way, towards another part of the castle and entering this magnificent room with a very long table, full of the most appealing food.

At the front of the table, was sitting Princess Marygolda, about eight years old, quite tall for that age, comparing it, to our eight years old from our world. She was surrounded by Una and Ella.

The Princess was wearing a bright gold and orange dress, all embroidered with all kinds of beautifully shinning stones and flowers; her hair of auburn colour and an almost transparent porcelain skin, and could see the little horns starting to grow, very pretty indeed, although she portrayed a melancholic look, especially on her dark eyes.

Adriana, proceeded towards the Princess, and with a bow, she started to introduce the group to her; for a moment the group saw her eye brightening up for the sight of this young and different people; she welcomed them to her realm and invited them to sit and to joying her for breakfast.

"Please sit with me!". She was quite friendly and easy to talk for a Princess (not that the group ever meet a real Princess anyway) and to Adriana's joy, that they were bonding with ease.

They talked more in details about their task, and they pledged to the Princess to do everything in their power to help her kingdom; the Princess with a smile then thanked them in advance and pledged herself, to do everything to help them too.

Halfway thru their breakfast, suddenly, the door opened and Euphenia entered, addressing the Princess good morning and ignoring the rest of the guests sitting there with her.

The Princess then asked Euphenia; "have you meet our guests?".

And with an evil look towards them, "No my lady, I haven't had the pleasure yet!". With a sarcastic answer.

Then she went behind each of them asking their names and paying attention specially to Elwin; He could feel her eyes on him almost like knives, trying to enter his mind to find out what Adriana wanted from them.

Adriana seeing Elwin discomfort, intervened. "We shall make our way out now!", breaking her grip on Elwin's mind and giving back a malicious look towards her.

Clearly, now everyone was feeling uncomfortable in Euphenia's presence. Princess Marygolda noticed that and asked Euphenia to leave and to see if the King felt better; with a bow to the Princess, she left the room, looking back at them with a painful grin.

The princess then apologised to the group and Adriana for the appalling attitude of her aunt. “We shall see you a dinner time, my lady!", Adriana said to the Princess, and with a courtesy bow they all leave the room. As soon as they get out, Oscar exclaimed; “what a breakfast!”, they all cracked in a laugh. “I’m sorry about Euphenia, she hasn’t got any manners and also, I need to warn you about her servant, Artier, do not trust him at all!” Adriana said to the group.

“Today, we will go to explore some of the places that I wish for you to see and you have to meet very special helpers!”, Adriana says, “oh yes, I definitely look forward to. Are you ready?”, Elwin said to the group.

With a nod and newfound strength, they agreed.

Making their way outside the castle, at the bottom of the staircase, Scarlet was waiting for them; “good morning!”, “how was your rest?”. “Very good, Scarlett thanks!”. Elwin replied.

“We have a bit of walk to get to the sacred place where the Stone Menhir are standing!” Adriana said.

Walking through the forest for about twenty minutes, they came to a clearing and there standing tall, very tall, a circle of stones, that they call the Nhoor Menhir; weathered and very ancient, about sixteen of them; they are surrounded by huge oaks and holm oaks in the valley of the river called Flumendosa, in the middle of two mountain slopes. The group was sensing the energy all around, powerful and positive.

Adriana then said to the group; “please enter the circle with me, one at the time!”; then Adriana, called Elwin to come nearer and to close his eyes. “Now, Elwin a creature will appear before you; you need it for as long you are staying here, a sort of a helper, familiar or friend, if you wish too; it can show to yourself as anything, even if you think it looks scary and dangerous, trust your feelings and instinct and let's hope that they will accept you too!" Adriana said; the group with a perplexed look, looked at each other.

"Don't worry too much!", Scarlett said, "they are here to guide and protect you, on your journey!".

Elwin with the help of Adriana to keep him steady, asked him to close his eyes and to concentrate.

A brilliant green light washed over him; he could feel the warmth, emanating from this light; he opened his eyes and standing before him, there it was, a majestic Dragon; with a shocked face and a bit scared by this incredible sight, he backed away a bit, but the feeling was positive and friendly.

Adriana then asked Elwin to bow and to introduce himself to him; "My name is Elwin!".

The Dragon, then bow back to Elwin and with a thundering voice, replied; "my name is Tiddraigh, protector of the forests!" Elwin, after his initial shock, got a very welcoming and positive feeling about Tiddraigh, and thanked it for choosing him.

He then moved out of the Stone Circle with Elwin following him.

Next was Aqua to enter the Stones circle; "please close your eyes, Aqua", Adriana says. A beautiful white light washed over her; opening her eyes, she's welcomed by a Unicorn, bright as the whitest fresh snow, then as Elwin did, she bowed to the Unicorn and said to it, "My name is Aqua, and I'm pleased to meet you!". The Unicorn bowed back at her, accepting her companionship.

"My name is Primara, 'the Just', and I'm pleased to meet you, Aqua." Aqua approached Primara and stroking her side.

Lunette was so excited to be the next one, jumping up and down.

Adriana held her hand while she entered the sacred circle.

An amazing golden light washed over her and as she opened her eyes, there stood before her a Centaur, then Lunette, exclaimed, "I can't believe this!" and as the other two did, bowed at him and introduced herself; the Centaur then bow back, "my name is Bolzac, watcher of the small creatures of the wild and I'm pleased to meet you!". Then they walked away out of the circle.

Adriana welcomed Alyssa into the circle.

Please close your eyes and concentrate. A stunning bright violet light appeared over Alyssa, touching her head first, and then after a few seconds, washed all over her.

Opening her eyes, she's met by a stunningly black giant wolf, with green eyes.

Alyssa, with joy, bowed after him and said: "I'm Alyssa!", the wolf almost immediately, bowed back at her, "My name is Amarok, 'guardian of the mountain's pass' and I'm pleased to be able to help you!". Adriana, nodded at Alyssa with consent and pride.

Finally, Oscar's time has arrived; all looking at him with excitement; "close your eyes, Oscar!". Adriana said; as he was concentrating, a bright blue light, washed over him, taking a bit longer to disappear.

He opened his eyes and there before him stood a great, strong huge bear; with his eyes open wide, Oscar bowed to the great bear and introduced himself.

The bear with an almighty roar, bowed back at him, "I'm Olbeonth, commander of the bears army, at your service!".

Then Adriana, stepped in the middle of the Great Stone circle, with open arms, thanking all the great magical creatures for choosing to help the group on their quest. "We all belong in this beautiful and peaceful realm, and I would like for all of you to stand next to each other, here inside the circle with me"; Adriana said, "we are about to receive a very important visit!"

So, in front of them, these bright lights came down from above, in a vertical line, so bright that was almost impossible to watch it with your naked eyes; it came down almost next to Adriana, but not touching the ground. There, appearing before them, three 'entities'.

The group noticed that Adriana and the rest of the magical creatures, bowed in front of them, so they did the same.

Alyssa, with discretion looked back and assumed that these entities must have been the Shining Ones. They were made from some sort of energy, with transparent bodies, much taller than all of them, even than Adriana and her fellows Perdaxius.

Adriana and the rest of the group looked in awe at the sight.

The Shining Ones didn't have any apparent features in their faces or body, just brilliant white light, like shinning diamonds all over, pure energy.

They communicated telepathically and they commanded respect and power but also you could feel the positive and wise energy, emanating from them.

"This is the group from the human world, my Lords!". Adriana said, they turned to look at the group and making a gesture to Elwin to come closer.

Elwin, with confidence and courage, stood before them.

"We are pleased to see you and your friends too!", "I am Aat, and this are Iset and Menek!".

Elwin, looking so mesmerized by this amazing sight, spoke to them in his mind, and thanked them, saying that it was an honour to be able to stand before them; taken by his humble gesture Iset, said, "You and your companions will face a very dangerous and hard task, but with our help, that of your familiars and Adriana, our joint forces will prevail against evil!". Menek, also said, "Don't forget, that you are all pure of heart and your powerful weapon in your Iag energy!".

Then, Aat asked the group to stand together in the middle of the Stones Circle. "Please close your eyes and join hands!".

The Shining Ones, then raised their hands and a beam of energy emanating from them as to form an orb, in which all the group was in. Adriana and the familiars looked in awe and seeing the group almost disappearing inside this stunningly bright light.

Without saying anything, the bright orb lifted up with all of them inside.

Everything around them was so bright and charged with pure positive energy. All of this commotion was attracting a lot of curious forest creatures and not only animals but also fairies, Undines, Gnomes and all the spirits of the forest, by the feeling emanating from all this positive energy.

The orb, slowly came down and the group, one by one opened their eyes; they remained speechless.

The Shining Ones explained to them that what they just experienced, was the awakening of their Iag Energy, that only young humans have, and it was necessary to give them extra protection and strength, against the creatures of the abyss, against their powerful dark magic.

Adriana, stepped in and thanking them for the powerful gift granted to them. The Shining Ones then disappeared in the sky, but everyone could hear the voice of one of them, it was Aat, “We shall meet again, very soon!”

Chapter Seven

'The dream'

The day was almost over. On the horizon, the sunset was getting blood red in colour and that was an omen that the creatures of darkness were nearby, attracted by all that positive energy around.

As almost had they finished looking at the sunset, a strident cry pierced the sky; the familiars were on full alert and all the other creatures that were around them, ran away hiding, into the deeps of the forest.

There, in the sky above them, the Evil Five, riding on top of Harpies, and followed by all manner of flying monsters, snake like and insect like, inbreeded with, what looks like, humans so corrupted by them and impossible to redeem them back to their true forms.

Elwin and the others were confused by that sight, and asking Adriana how those creatures came to be. "They are corrupted ancient Elves!".

She explained that some of the creatures of darkness, were able to get to the human world and kidnap some of them for evil intent and, with a solemn face, also for food, leaving the group horrified by that notion.

Adriana and the familiars gathered around the group in a circle to protect them. Elwin and Alyssa, said, "we must fight them Adriana, we are ready to help you!", "give us a chance to prove ourselves!", Oscar said, "No, you're not ready, yet!", Adriana replied.

Then, the Evil Five, with at the front their leader, Aeldry, suddenly stopped, hoovering almost on top of them, to the group's surprise. "They're testing us, they must have felt the energy of the Shining Ones!" Amarok said.

"Shame, I was ready for some barbecue Harpies!" Tiddraigh added. Adriana and the group looked at him and smiled. Aeldry, looked straight into Elwin's eyes, recognising him as the group's leader.

A chill run up on his spine and for a good reason too; the Evil Five were not to be underestimated, specially Aeldry; "she is a master of mental torture!", Bolzac, said; I lost my father to her, bowing his head. She tortured him to death, for not bowing to the 'Dark One'!"

"I was there, long ago and I could't do anything to help him!" He added.

Adriana approached Bolzac.

"It wasn't your fault, we will honour Balur's memory, very soon!".

After all the noise and show off, the Evil five left, taking with them all the entourage of flying monsters.

It was time to get back to the castle. Elwin and the others had to say goodbye to their respective familiars, asking Adriana when they were going to meet again. "We shall meet up again, tomorrow at noon, we need to make sure that the armours are ready for battle!"

As Adriana finished to talk, Aqua asked her; "armours?". "What kind of armours they need to wear!". Aqua continue. "You shall see them tomorrow, Aqua!". Adriana added.

Tiddraigh with his thunderous voice said, "see you tomorrow, and remember that, it doesn't matter how small you are to make a difference in the lives of others; a positive future for our worlds, and any world!".

He then lifted his body up with his huge wings, making everyone holding each other to keep steady from the strong wind with everyone looking the majestic creature, disappearing in the night. The others did the same going in different directions thru the forest, leaving Adriana and the group there.

Elwin and the others, by now, were in a thoughtful mood and some of them, still in disbelieve, but excited that they would be fighting very soon together with Adriana and all those amazing creatures, that they could call them friends.

Back at the castle and in their rooms, the group were a bit shocked and horrified by the thought of the kidnappings in their world, and for that awful purpose. "Absolutely shocking!"

Aqua said.

"So all those disappearances that we hear all the time, some must be by them!". She added.

Oscar mentioned a story that he's Grandfather used to tell him.

"A man in his neighbourhood, which was considered an eccentric and a bit mad, used to say that 'Monsters', had tried to get to him in the night and no one would believe him; he started to do some drawings of this creatures that he saw, and one day he disappeared for sure, living only those drawings as witnesses, depicting those creatures that we had seen, some flying ones, half vulture, half human and some limbless lizard/snake likes!".

Continuing,

"I saw those drawings once and they were terrifying, but at the same time they attracted my curiosity!"

"What's happened to them?", Elwin asked; Oscar nodding in a disappointing, "don't know!". "I would have loved to see them!" Alyssa said.

"Now that I saw those creatures earlier on, I can recall similarities to those drawings!", Oscar, said. "Come on, guys we need to rest, tomorrow is going to be a very busy day, full of challenging tasks and we need all the strength!", Lunette, said, "we also have each other and we will stick together, always!", Elwin added.

Elwin sleep was troubled by a dark dream. 'In his vision he was on top of a hill, alone, in the night, strangely quiet and cold; there he was, standing in front of him, a huge black stone platform and in the middle, was an enormous black monolith.

Aeldry, the leader of the Evil Five, was there too, next to the huge black stone monolith, on the left side of this platform, looking at him, but without saying anything.

Suddenly raising her left hand and mumbling indecipherable words to him. The clear sky, in a matter of minutes became even darker by those ominous clouds; the winds were picking up and the ground was trembling, like an earthquake, then almost in front of him, the ground was cracking open…'

His sleep was interrupted by the glorious sun entering from the windows and made even more stunning by the little fairies, flying around and catching the rays on theirs wings, reflecting the light around the room in a kaleidoscope way.

After refreshing themselves up, the group headed to the kitchen for a spot of breakfast.

On the way there, Adriana joined them to the kitchen. Madame Bijoux, was already there, and giving them the warmest welcome and good morning, with the food, beautifully presented, and already on the table.

While they were eating, Adriana, looking at them, asked if they had any dreams or visions during the night.

Elwin, with a solemn face, bowed his head and nodded yes, to Adriana. “So, Elwin, would you like to talk about your dream?”. Elwin, looking straight into her beautiful and reassuring eyes, described the dream to her and the uncomfortable presence of Aeldry being there, also mentioning that he had a similar dream before coming to the Shardana world, at his house in Borghmorlock. “It was like a continuation of my previous dream back home!” he said.

Adriana explained to Elwin that the power of thc cvil five was very strong and that meant, that Aeldry want to test and scare you, the reason being, it’s because they’re themselves scared of all of you, specially you Elwin and your Iag Energy.

Then, Elwin interrupted Adriana, remembering that when the ground was shaking in the dream, he felt an indescribable darkness, followed by a fear that he never felt before.

A fear of the unknown, a fear of losing grip on reality.

“Yes, Elwin, you felt the dark energy of ‘the Dark One’. It was probably sensing yours too, but on the contrary of his dark one, yours is a bright and powerful, the Iag Energy, and ‘It is curious to see your capabilities.”

Elwin, amazed and curious of this gift that he supposed to have, also reassured by Adriana words, stood up and said to all; “Come on guys, I’m ready for another exciting day of learning!”.

“So were we’re going today, Adriana?” Alyssa said. “Today we’all explore further down the borders of Zinnigha Perdaxa, and I would like all of you to visit some villages, where the inhabitants consider themselves neutral, to either our world and the dark one, and I hope to speak with the elders of the villages to gain their trust and convince them, at least, to keep an eye on the borders of Hellebore Forest." "You see!", Adriana speaking to the group, "remember when I said that we need a certain degree of darkness in this world, and matter of fact in any world, to function, and there isn't a better place that Hellebore Forest to see this relationship between the dark and the light; creatures and entities that are happy to live in a perpetual twilight zone and manage to remain neutral to it!"

So, the group headed outside, after saying goodbye to the Princess. "Follow me!", Adriana said, leading them to the Nhoor Menhir, where the standing stones were located.

"Now, all of you must go with each of your familiars and we'll all meet up in the village of Guneria; don't worry, your familiars know the way!", she added.

Just before getting on their familiars, Aqua, asked Adriana, who lived in the Guneria village. "They're Forest Trolls, benevolent ones, but they're very unpredictable, sometimes they can be trouble maker!". Adriana replied. Oscar, then said, "I thought that Trolls, wouldn't be able to stand day light?". "Are they not turning into stone!". Lunette added.

"No, not the Forest Trolls!" Adriana said,

"They're able to live in villages in the open, a bit similar to some of your villages back in your world, just a bit messier, but they have great connection and understanding of the forest and their surroundings in which they live, in a way that they're so interwound with it, that they could't live without it.

We will meet the most powerful and influential elder General in the village, his name is Orcu, it's not going to be an easy meeting, but let's hope that he is in a good mood today!".

“Are there different types of Trolls here? I thought that they were all the same!”

Oscar asked Adriana.

“Yes, Oscar, here in the land of Shardana, live many different types of creatures, as for the Trolls concerned, the forest’s trolls are the most benevolent and peaceful ones; also, we have the cave Trolls, which as the Swamp ones, are the most dangerous and not to be trusted at all, especially the Swamp Trolls, that are the largest ones of their race and servant of the Dark One and the Necromancer.”

Chapter Eight

'The Guneria village'

As the group was looking around for their familiars, they could see in the distance, towards Hellebore Forest, the skies were dark and ominous and in the midst of it, some of the flying creatures that they saw in the company of Aeldry. "We must hurry!", Adriana said.

Elwin greeted Tiddraigh with excitement to the idea of riding a dragon; Tiddraigh bowed his head and neck for Elwin to climb up and securing himself, holding with his hands on two of Tiddraigh horns on his neck and with a thunderous roar; Tiddraigh lifted his huge wings and took off to the sky.

The group looked on, in awe to this amazing sight. The rest of the group greeted the respective familiars; Aqua, on top of Primara, as Lunette and Alyssa with Bolzac and Amarok.

Oscar before getting on Olbeonth, looked perplexed at Adriana and asked her. "How you're going to get to Guneria village, Adriana?", with a smile and thanking Oscar for his concern, she turned to look in the undergrowth and there it was before them a huge wild boar appears grunting, "this is my friend Onik and he'll give me a lift to Guneria village!" Adriana added.

Now, everyone was ready to proceed towards Guneria village and starting to make their way through the forest. Although being a dark and densely wooded, with huge and very old trees, Hellebore Forest got his own charm and fascination. They reached a stone bridge, crumbling and very old. Adriana, explained to the group, that the river flowing trough was Riu Marigosu. Alyssa then said, "Oh my, this river goes all the way to the underworld, isn't it?", "Yes Alyssa!", Adriana replied.

"So, please everyone, be careful and watch your surroundings, because some creature from the underworld uses it to move around in the forest and would attack and kidnap anyone who's got to close to the shores specially in the darker areas or in their way, to bring them to the...", without letting Adriana finish her sentence, Oscar, added, "for the Dark One, isn't it?", almost at the same time, a huge black snake, came out from the shores of the dark waters.

Standing straight, with a menacing posture. "Quick, move over here!" Bolzac, shouted the group. The huge snake with a hiss, promptly lounged towards Lunette. Bolzac, armed with a bow and arrow, launched himself in between them, firing an arrow at the snake, that with a hiss of pain moved a bit back.

Oscar, armed with a broken branch that was laying on the ground next to him, hit the snake straight in the snout, making it to shake his head in distress; then, the huge beast, tail first, slid back into the dark waters, pausing for a moment and with his eyes darker than the darkest night, looked back straight into Oscar eyes.

At the same time, Oscar felt a chill running through his body as if that was not going to be the last time, that he would encounter the beast. The familiars were amazed and proud of their courage and said to Adriana that they needed their armours and weapons, and in a hurry.

Adriana agreed with them, with a bow of approval.

Olbeonth, with his deep voice, said, "We must carry on, and not wasting any time, to our way to the village!".

"Yes, we must!", Adriana added. "We are almost there!", Amarok, said.

The entrance of the Guneria village was flanked by two huge oak trees, twisted into an almost a door and guarded by two large Troll. Olbeonth and Bolzac approached them and calling their names. "Rdor, Oid, how are you? Long time without seeing you guys!", with an answer that resembled more of a grunting than a welcome, the two guards welcomed them in the village and said that Orcu was expecting them.

Adriana was not so surprised by that the forest Trolls were in possession of a powerful sacred well, in which the elders of the village could use it for foresight; this well was old as the forest itself, was called Morthold and very important to the forest Trolls, it was guarded by the High Priestess Maxima.

Rdor showed with a gesture the way to the main square where Orcu's dwelling was located.

On the way there, the group was looking at the rest of the village, which was quite big and buzzing with all kinds of trolls, big and small and other different creatures all around.

"Guneria, it is an important village for trade in these parts of the north of Hellebore Forest, and attracts all sort of creatures, that some are very unsavoury and some dangerous, so be careful, keep your eyes open and be on your guard at all the time!", Adriana said.

Finally, they reached a large square; Elwin and Tiddraigh were already there waiting for them.

In the middle of it, there was a large round building, made of gigantic granite stones, with all kinds of plants growing all over it.

They dismounted their familiars, and they stayed outside the stone building standing guard, with Olbeonth and Amarok having a chat with their friends Rdor and Oid, the rest of the familiars were not that amused by that, especially when all those little young trolls surrounded them, looking at the group with curiosity.

This huge Troll came out of the building, not very welcoming and graceless; Adriana, with a bow introduced the group to him; "This is Orcu, the great General of the forest Trolls race of the North." "Yes, I'm Orcu and I know why you're here!", he said, looking towards Adriana. "Thank you for seeing us Orcu and I bring to you and your people, greetings from our dear King Niuxs VI and Princess Marygolda, and as you said, there isn't much that I can say, that you already know!".

Orcu, with his fierce look, sighed and bowed his head, saying:

"Yes, we're starting to have serious problems with them too and as you know, we're not great friends either, but it's much easier to live along with your kind, the Perdaxiusu, than to deal with the dark ones!". The group liked his honesty and clarity. "Can I ask what are the problems that you and your people are experiencing?" Adriana said.

Arren, Orcu's wife, then interrupted and welcomed them inside their home, and gesturing to sit on some wooden chairs around the fire, which was in the middle of the building, burning fiercely and noisily. Adriana thanked Arren for her hospitality.

The stone building was of a round construction with all around many other passages that led to other smaller rooms, in which all sort of smaller trolls came in and out, busy with the daily chores and bringing some food for the guests. "You see Adriana, the Evil Five, are kidnapping our young ones, to be used as slaves or to be trained for the battlefield, this is happening all over Hellebore forest, and not only with our race, but with all the other races that dwell here in this forest and the surroundings area; we can't let them continue with this insult!".

Then Orcu, looking behind Adriana, asked. "And what exactly are these funny looking creatures?". "They're from the other world and…!", without letting Adriana finish her sentence. "Humans?" Orcu said standing up from his huge chair and with an almost disgust towards them. "What are you going to do with this bunch of useless humans?" he spoke.

Adriana, annoyed and a bit embarrassed by that awkward assumption; replied to him,

"That those 'humans' were the weapons to help balancing our world!". Orcu, cracking a laughs, "please, give me a reason to believe you, Adriana!"

Putting her hand over Orcu's arm and giving the back to the others for a bit of privacy, Adriana whispered to Orcu, that the Shining One had detected an unusual energy around them, especially on Elwin, something that they never felt before here in Shardana, calling it, 'the Iag', a kind of alive, primordial energy, amazingly powerful, "why are you keeping them in the dark about it?" Orcu said to Adriana. "It's for their own safety at the moment, we need to help them, on to develop and control this energy together, making it more powerful and long lasting!". Orcu with a serious face, looking and listening very careful at Adriana, said, "I apologise for my behaviour toward the humans and you can count on us Adriana!", "I'all gather all the other races in the Hellebore Forest and around it, and try to convince some of them, to join us on this quest!".

"Thank you Orcu!" Adriana said, "but be aware that isn't going to be easy, especially with the 'Shadow Fairies', as you know, Adriana, they're very unpredictable and dangerous!". "Yes, I'm aware of them Orcu, and aware that they possess a very powerful item, that we will need!". "The Ring of the Dead?", Orcu replied. "It's a very dangerous relic from the ancient times, Adriana, and only the Shadow Fairies's High Priestess Mircalla, can control it!", "can we trust her?" He added. "Only time will answer that question and maybe somebody else, that may be able to control the Ring of the Dead too!", Adriana replied, looking towards Alyssa.

"We're going to leave now, Orcu, and I thank you and Arren for your time and help from all Perdaxiusu and we shall meet Maxima another time!" Adriana said; Orcu bowed his head in agreement and followed them outside in the village's square. Elwin approached him and looking straight in his eyes, telling him that he wouldn't be disappointed by a 'human', also thanking him for listening and trusting them; Orcu with a surprised face, in seeing this little people, so confident and sure of themselves, that his feelings were right to give them a chance to help to save their land.

Chapter Nine

'The armours'

On their way to get their armours trough Hellebore Forest, Alyssa noticed some shadows around them. "Can you all see those shadows?" "They have faces!", Alyssa said to the group; but no onc apart from her, could see them. They only saw some sort of faint smoky shadows moving around.

Adriana stopped and explained that the Shadow Fairies were around them and that they're masters of disguise; they come and go like the wind. "They're checking on us!"

Primara said; "Alyssa, you're able to sense and see them, I had my suspicion on that!", Adriana said. "What do you mean Adriana!" Alyssa replied.

"In your world you're able to see and sense the souls of the dead and that explained why you're able to see them here too, because the Shadow Fairies are able to shift from the world of the living and the world of the dead with ease!". Adriana added that if Orcu had not much luck with Mircalla, "I think I should take you to meet the High Priestess!".

They went back to the Nhoor Menhir where some of the Perdaxiusu were waiting for the group with all the amours ready for them.

They all dismounted their familiars to gather around the Stone Circle, admiring the fine work done on the armours.

The metal workers were the Dwarves from the caves of Monte e'Zinnigha, as most of the Perdaxiusu couldn't touch the metal and the Dwarves had a greater skill on working with any kind of metal. Adriana invited Elwin first into the circle, she was followed by some Dwarves to help handing to him his armour. It was made of a dark gold colour, with dragon motifs to compliment his alliance with Tiddraigh; "This armour is made to withstand any kind of fire or heat source, Elwin!", Adriana said "may this protect you!", she added.

Next was Alyssa to be invited into the circle when at the same time the dark shadows appeared again around Alyssa, but this time were more tangible and solid, so that all the group could see them clearly. In the middle of them, this beautiful fairy appeared.

Her skin white as the freshly picked snowdrops; her hair and eyes, black as the darkest night in the winter months. She approached Alyssa and introduced herself as Mircalla; Adriana, pleased by this unexpected visit, welcomed Mircalla to the standing Stones and supposing that she had already talked to Orcu.

"Adriana, I was there all the time when you and the group were in Orcu's dwelling, and heard everything, although, I wouldn't mind to have a chat in private with that grumpy old Troll, on calling me and my kind, unpredictable and dangerous!". Adriana bowed her head in a consenting gesture and a smile. "You are very welcome High Priestess of the Shadow Fairies!" she added.

Then Mircalla, approached Alyssa offering her the armour and while both of their hands touched, there was some sort of electric static, that confirmed Mircalla that Alyssa was well deserving from their help and protection. Alyssa not only was stunned by their trust on her but finding out that the Shadow Fairies, could touch metal without arming them.

Alyssa armour was, as you can expect, made by a shinning black metal, with all around, some kind of runic symbols. Mircalla explained that they were protection spells for her and Amarok. Alyssa thanked Mircalla, for her trust.

Mircalla with a smile and the other fairies disappeared as quickly as they appeared.

The group and everyone around were in shock, knowing how difficult was to deal with the Shadow Fairies, especially Adriana and the familiars, that thanked Alyssa for her steadiness.

Aqua was the next one, followed by Primara at her side; a dwarf handed her the armour, ~~in~~ which was of an ivory colour, with wings all over the top plates.

Aqua, impressed by all the beauty of the armour, asked what was the meaning of the wings. One of the Dwarves, stepped in and explained that if she wished, could use the armour for flying.

Thanking the Dwarf, aqua asked his name and if it was one of his creations. "My name is Mordrek, and yes, this is my creation, is a pleasure to serve you!". "Thank you Mordrek!"

Aqua replied with a shy smile, reciprocated by him.

Lunette couldn't wait to get her armour and almost tripped on a root that was sticking up from the ground. Followed by Bolzac, that in this case offered her the armour.

Made by the purest silver, blessed by the Sacred Ladies of Simieri, inlaid by scene of ancient battles, celebrating the victories of Bolzac's father, Balur the great.

"It's an honour to wear this armour Bolzac!", Lunette said.

Bolzac with a bow, thanked her and replied that was an honour too to be part of this group.

Finally, Oscar, that as usual was the gentleman of the group and waited patiently for his turn. Accompanied by Olbeonth at his side, Adriana watched with a smile, while two dwarves gave to him his armour. A strong coppery colour one, with in the centre a bear face design to honour the great race of the Bear's Armies.

Oscar with a big hug, thanked Olbeonth, who at the same time was surprised and pleased by that.

Elwin looked at Oscar with joyful eyes and thinking that he liked him even more, seeing his special friend so confident for the better and in such short time, at the same time Oscar felt Elwin looking at him and smiled back.

Adriana welcomed the group and their familiars, back inside the Nhoor Menhir, for another special visit.

Here again from the sky above the Shining Ones appeared, emanating such a bright and positive lights.

Aat pleased to see them all sorted and almost ready, joined hands with Iset and Menek, inviting Adriana in the centre too. Reciting at the same time a special spell of strength and protection in thunderous voices, the spell begun.

"I Aat, I Iset, I Menek

send the purest positive lights from the deepest
regions of the Universe

to protect and give strength to these brave warriors and
their helpers, always be"

Everyone was enveloped by the brightest lights that anyone has ever seen, at least by any human for that matter.

As before, all this energy attracted so many creatures from the forest near the Stones Circle, curious and amazed by all this positive energy.

Amongst them in the background, some of Aeldry's spies and servant of the Dark One, checking what was going on, but for some of them, all this positive bright light was too much to bear, recoiling in pain and discomfort, running away into the depths of the darkest area of the forest and one in particular in the castle direction; after about ten minutes, the lights went dimmer, and the Shining Ones stopped.

Adriana, noticed that also in the background behind an old tree trunk, there she was, Euphenia, with her face twisted in pain and in disbelief, just now realising how blind she was of Adriana's plans; with a terrifying screech she took off to the sky, stopping in midair, cursing the group and Adriana, challenging them to dare to stop her and the Dark One with the forces of darkness.

She then transformed herself into a magpie and flew away in the opposite direction of the castle.

Everyone was shocked by Euphenia's reaction but the one who wasn't impressed at all, was Adriana, because she knew very well, how evil and opportunistic Euphenia was.

The Shining Ones kept silent after the spell, and gesture to all the group to gather around and to be prepared, because Euphenia and the Dark One, just declared war to all the bright side creatures of this world and beyond.

"Now, is very important to train as fast as we can, our very important friends for battle!"

Aat said. "You must be strong!". Menek added. "Now go and rest, because you need all the strength that you can get!", Iset, said. "Remember, we're always a thought away!" Aat added.

With a wind whirl, they just disappeared into the sky. But Adriana, had other plans before they went to the castle to eat and rest.

Chapter Ten

'The Dark One'

The skies were dark and menacing, the winds strong and cold. A lonely and bitter Euphenia was heading to the wastelands of Vernus, across the waters in between Riu Marigosu and the Dark Sea, where perpetual twilight was reigning.

Stopping on top of this immense dark rock, Euphenia regaining her true form, screamed with rage and disappointment with herself for not foreseen this outcome. She knew that now was impossible to get back to Zinnigha Perdaxa, as her carefully cover was blown away.

All around her, creatures of the shadow emerged from cracks in the rocks and the undergrowth. From the distance, a swirl of blackness approached her, and from it, Aeldry and the Evil Five appeared. "Welcome back to Vernus, Euphenia!", Aeldry said;

With a look that could kill. "Are you joking, we have work to do!", Euphenia said.

"Take me to the Dark One!" she added.

Aeldry and the others, with a smirk obliged, knowing that when anyone disagreed with her, had to pay severe consequences.

They approached a low bank in the swamps with a huge crumbling and rotting ruins, a very large square building, with no apparent windows and with only one entrance. Flanked on each side, by two giant swamp

Trolls, with a very bad attitude and not too fond of the Evil Five.

Grunting and swinging their wooden clubs, stopping the Evil Five in their tracks and letting only Euphenia pass.

Inside the building, was drier, so Euphenia could walk instead of flying; all around her, there were all sort of creatures, deformed and seemingly in a constant suffering state, as Euphenia's brightness was around them and not having a care for creating them discomfort. Even if she was consumed by evil, being part of the Coven Iroxi, meant that she's still retained the brightness of the Coven.

The main door was opened by more Swamp Trolls, letting out a humid, putrid stench with flies and all sort of crawlies, all around, that made her step back a bit.

There, in the middle of this gigantic room, was situated a throne, made by pointed and rusting metal pieces, interwoven with the crashed bones of the creatures of the bright side, that were unfortunate in off, to be captured and eaten by them and their remains used for this awful spectacle.

Among them, Euphenia notice some of the bones were from the world of humans and with a pleasurable thought, thinking that Elwin and the rest of the group, would be a fitting addiction to the throne.

On each side of this despicable throne, there were two entities, created by the Dark One's Necromancer, with no name, a revolting and the most unpleasant and dangerous creature in Vernus, after the Dark One.

Her heart, if she had one, was so dark that, not even next to the Shining Ones, would come to light. Even Euphenia, feared her as she was very ancient and powerful witch and the Dark One's favourite.

The air was tense, and the energy was building up.

Still no sign of the Dark One. Then an echoing and deep laugh sounded all around, with the two entities facing at each other and raising their emaciated hand. The Necromancer appeared from behind the throne; a very scary looking ancient witch, almost like a deformed mix of a dwarf and a goblin, hunchbacked and with protruding eyes, with no expression and lifeless as she was already dead.

Euphenia tried to remain still and confident and not to show any fear, but the Necromancer, could 'cut' trough like a knife with her mind, just by looking, and feeling a touch of fear from Euphenia, making her smirking with pleasure.

In the middle of the throne, a black mass was raising up, then, there it was in front of them, the Dark One; Euphenia and the rest of the creature inside the room, were kneeling down and not daring to look up, finally he talked, welcoming her to Vernus.

Raising her face and looking into the Dark One's eyes for the first time in her long life, was surprisingly not a scary sight to Euphenia; he was a giant, and in a humanoid form, larger than anything that she ever seen it before, even larger than all the Swamp Trolls around him, but his energy was different, emanating pure evil, a kind of unspeakable and sinister evil.

His eyes were a burning shade of blue; his skin was almost like black charcoal colour, with strikes of molten lava emanating a blue fire all around his body. His presence commanded fear and a sort of twisted respect.

"Euphenia, came closer to me!". The Dark One said. "You've been a faithful servant to me!", he added. Euphenia with a pleased face, but with a dash of fear, not knowing what his reaction would be, after all the disappointing events that had happened earlier; "Thank you my Lord, always a pleasure to serve the Dark One!", she added.

"Your loyalty pleases me, and I want to entrust you with my armies, to march to the bright side of Shardana and bring them to the dark side and under my control!"; with a shocked face, Euphenia bowed her head in agreement; not that she had any choice; "also, I want you to take charge of some of the Armies of the Ancient Dead!", looking at the same time down to the Necromancer, to see what her reaction would be.

She didn't look too pleased but, with an evil grin, that would scare even the most seasoned Swamp Troll, she had no choice, but to agree to the Dark One request.

Chapter Eleven

'The Dwarves of Monte e'Zinnigha'

Elwin and the group were heading back to the castle, with a sombre and a bit worried feeling. Oscar stopped and approached Elwin, taking his hands into his and looking into his eyes. "Hey Elwin, we're all in on this together!" Oscar said, and gesturing to rest of the group to come closer and to get a hug together.

Adriana and the familiars, with joy and pride, looked at these five young brave future warriors and joining them around. "Sorry to interrupt, but before we get to the castle, I would like to take all of you, to meet a very important Perdaxiu!", Adriana said.

"Who would that be, Adriana?" Alyssa added.

"She's a very old and wise Dwarf High Priestess, Mobromora from Monte e'Zinnigha, keeper of one of the most important and ancient Sacred Wells, very different from all the others in Shardana, in which all are scattered around in the open, inside the forests or high in the mountains, this one is unique because is the only one situated inside the deepest regions of the caves and hold the very primordial waters, old as Shardana itself!".

"Mobromora? One of the elders that you mention earlier on Adriana?" Alyssa said. "Yes, Alyssa!" Adriana added.

So even if everyone was tired, they were still curious and excited to go and meet her.

Tiddraigh was the only one a bit concerned and Adriana knew why; "What is the matter Tiddraigh?", Elwin asked him.

The dark caves of Monte e'Zinnigha held some dark memories in his life. "You see, Elwin, long ago, before the Dwarves took possession of the caves, Mountain Trolls dwelled inside it!".

Taking a deep breath, as everyone was looking at each other waiting for him to continue.

"The Cave Trolls took some of my siblings, when still very small and not be able to defend themselves yet, I and one of my sisters only, escaped by hiding behind some rocks and leaves!". "What happed to them?", Aqua said, "We do not know, but I don't think anything good for that matter!", Tiddraigh replied.

Elwin approached Tiddraigh and putting his hand over his chest; "we're always with you!", he spoke.

After this sad moment, Lunette asked Tiddraigh what was his sister's name and where she was now.

"She's called Fera, the Fierce, and I believe she's in the Northern Lands, at the edge of Shardana!". Tiddraigh replied.

"We will have the pleasure to meet her soon, very soon!", Adriana added with a warm smile, towards Tiddraigh.

The sun was still high in the sky, and as always in the distance towards the Vernus lands, the sky was dark and forbidding.

So, the group made their way towards the caves of Monte e'Zinnigha, to meet the High Priestess of the Sacred Well, Mobromora.

Before approaching the caves, the group had to climb a slope with a narrow, twisting road.

The air became colder as they climbed higher, turning on their left side, there it was, the entrance of the caves of the Kingdom of the Dwarves of Monte e'Zinnigha.

A quite large reinforced door, for a Dwarfing place, with no one in sight, guarding it.

"No one it's home?" Oscar said, jokingly; and before Adriana could said anything, the heavy door with a creaking sound, opened.

Two Dwarves guards, heavily armoured and with weapons on the ready, standing at each side of the entrance, making space for Monte e'Zinnigha cave's Prince Mordrek.

"I and Queen Afresial III welcomes you to the caves of Monte e'Zinnigha!" Mordrek, said.

Aqua and the group, were in shock, realising that the Dwarf who helped them to make the beautiful armours, was in fact a Prince.

"Please, don't stand there and follow me inside," giving a smile towards Aqua, who smiled back at him.

Tiddraigh and the other familiars, as expected, were not able to get inside, being so large, for the caves.

Then Adriana, suggested the familiars, if they wished, they were free to leave and they would meet up the following day for the training of the group.

They agreed and bowing to each other, left.

Elwin and the others looked while they familiars and friends left, with a sad feeling.

As the group followed Mordrek inside, they were meet with astonishment in realising how big the caves were and full of life; Oscar also saying that their familiars could have gotten inside with them. Adriana, touching his arm and with a smile saying, "It's better this way, Oscar!".

Confused by that assumption, they carried on following Mordrek down a flight of steps, going deeper and deeper into the caves. At the end of the tunnel, they could see some bright lights, but not made by the torches spread all over the cave walls in the upper rooms, these ones were different and as soon as they got inside this large and high walls room, they realised, what was emanating the lights.

All over the stone walls, there was a kind of mossy plants and ferns, glowing, pulsating and making this place look alive.

In between the stone, the moss and the ferns, there was all kind of little creatures, black and red salamanders slithering around, shinning metallic black and blue spiders and very small bright flying creatures.

In the middle of it, there it was, the Sacred Well, beautifully kept, and with the same wall plants all over is edges.

The more you came nearer, the more you could hear a sound, a humming sound, but very relaxing and a kind of comforting energy.

All of them mesmerised by this dream like place, looking around, when from the recesses of the room on the right-hand side, a figure appeared; Adriana, gestured the group to bow their heads and introduce them, the High Priestess of the Sacred Well of Monte e'Zinnigha. "This is Mobromora, and we thank you and yours people for seeing us, in this very dark times!", Adriana said, "and I welcome you Adriana and the group to our temple!",

Mobromora, added.

Mobromora was a jolly looking old dwarf lady, with a red dress and an over coat in dark leather with red inserts on the rims; also wearing an apron with blue square design, with all sort of items hanging on it, like amulets. Her hair of a dark reddish tone, long and plated with gold pins and rings. Holding on her right hand, a twisted staff with set on top of it, a huge green emerald.

Walking slowly, giggling and smiling all the way to Adriana, that had to nil to be able to embrace her; "I'm so happy, that you came here before setting for battle!", she said. "You know Mobromora, that we cannot fight with the armours alone!", Adriana added.

"Yes, yes, that is why we need to hurry and test the group!" Mobromora said.

"Test the group?", Elwin asked. "Gather around the edge of the well everyone, and you'll see what we mean about testing you!". Mobromora, replied.

With Adriana stepping back and letting the group nearer the well, Mobromora started chanting and getting in a sort of trans, with the lights all around them, getting brighter; coming out of the glowing moss, little translucent fairies of pure light, buzzing all over the group; then, Mobromora, raised her staff and from the Emerald jewel, emanating a green orb of light that incorporated all five of them herself included.

There from inside the Sacred Well, one at the time, five wooden staffs emerged from the waters, in which the little fairies handed to each of them.

Oscar looked a bit disappointed, because he was wishing for a sword but never believed that would be ending up with a piece of wood.

The staffs had some differences from each other; Elwin's one was made from a walnut wood with a beautiful ruby at the top; Alyssa's one was made from a Rowan wood and on top of hers was a Black Onyx.

Aqua was next to receive her staff, which was made from pomegranate wood and on top there was a white quartz, similar as the one Adriana gave to her. "At least, I got double protection! "Aqua said, with Adriana and Mobromora smiling.

Lunette's one was made from chestnut wood and on her one a pale blue angelite.

Finally, Oscar's staff was made from oak wood and on top a blue moonstone and has Aqua's one, Lunette and Oscar's too, were given by Adriana earlier in their journey.

With their staffs in their hands, the group were studying their new additions. "You now have to give your weapons a name; a name that only you must know and keep secret even amongst each other!", Mobromora said.

Everyone was thinking fast, and Mobromora giggling, interrupted them and assuring that they have a bit of time to name it and must be done on your own, with a clear mind.

Thanking Mobromora and Prince Mordrek for their hospitality and help. Alyssa then said,

"I wished to have meet the Queen Afresial III!", "Don't worry Alyssa, you will meet her majesty soon!", Adriana, replied.

Heading outside the caves with Adriana, the day was getting dark and all the group, although very tired, were so excited and already thinking for a name for the staffs.

On the way down from the caves towards the castle, Oscar took the courage and asked Adriana, what she meant about our familiars not be able to get inside the caves. "Dear Oscar, I didn't want Tiddraigh to see where his siblings went missing and bringing to him painful memories, so the rest of the familiars, out of respect for him, also decided not to get in!"

"So, did they really die, Adriana?" Elwin said.

"I don't think this is the moment and the place to dwell on this matter!" Adriana replied to him.

“Now, let’s hurry up to the castle, because, I’m sure you must be starving and there are lots of others, that want to meet all of you tonight at the feast prepared by the King!”

She added.

“A feast!” Oscar said. “Yes, Oscar the King wants to welcome you properly, because he wasn’t able too, when you meet him for the first time!” Adriana added.

“We’re looking forward to meet him again and to see who else is there, that we haven’t meet yet!”, Alyssa said, with all the rest of the group agreeing with her.

Chapter Twelve

'Styriax'

Back at the castle, Princess Marygolda was waiting to have dinner with them and had a surprise too, the King also was joining the group, feeling much better since Euphenia left the castle and her grip on him was getting wicker and wicker by the day.

"I have to apologise to you!" . The King said to the group.

"I wasn't myself when you first met me, due to…!", he paused for a moment;

"You know now!", he added.

King Niuxs VI and Princess Marygolda had prepared for them an opulent feast, to know each other better, but also with the rest of the Perdaxiusu and all the others that have been invited to the banquet, especially the ones that have to join them for the fight against the dark forces.

The feast was located in the grand hall of the Palace, with at the front in a U shape a very large table. A beautiful music and singing were being played by little fairies flying around the grand hall.

At the top of the table in the middle was sitting the King, with Princess Marygolda on the left and on his right there was sitting Euphenia, been related to the King, but for the first time the honour was bestowed to Adriana, for her unshakeable loyalty to the Kingdom of Zinnigha Perdaxa. Elwin was sitting next to Richard, which mentioned him that the Ections guards, were not able to get to battle with them, because were bound for the protection of the castle, but he could be on your side, as always. “You can count on me, Elwin!” Richard added. “Thanks Richard!”, Elwin replied.

Also present at the feast were other familiar faces to the group. The Dwarves of Monte e’Zinnigha caves, the Prince Mordrek and his mother Queen Afresial III, accompanied by the High Priestess of the Sacred Well, Mobromora and an entourage of loud dwarves.

Finally, Alyssa had the chance to meet the Queen, in which she picked up a melancholic aura about her majesty. “Isn’t she beautiful Queen Afresial III?“, Alyssa said to the group; with Madame Bijoux, adding, “the Queen is still heartbroken by the loss of her husband, the King Onanius V, slained in the battle for the control and protection of the mines of Monte e’Zinnigha.

“Mordrek was very young when he lost his father and grew ever close to his mother, in which he became a very fine and just Prince that one day will make a great King, thanks to his mother’s love!”, Madame Bijoux, added. “I’ll tell you the story, what happened on that dreadful day, another time when we’re alone!”, Madame Bijoux added.

Mircalla, the High Priestess of the shadow fairies was there too, with the old and wise Mother of all the Shadow Fairies, Styriax a very powerful and ancient fairy.

Orcu from the Guneria village was also present at the table with his usual grumpy attitude but not very happy to be there, as the food in the castle supposed to be a plant base one, so, the King made an exception for his very powerful allies and meat was on the menu for them. The Dwarves too were very happy to be able to have meat on the table.

Orcu was accompanied by his wife, Arren, a complete opposite of him, a jolly and friendly Forest Troll and quite pretty as a troll female can be and his personal guards, Rdor and Oid were there too. Also, the High Priestess Maxima was present so the group could meet her too; "she doesn't look very jolly like Orcu, but I guess is the Forest Trolls attitude!", Lunette whispering to Oscar, giggling.

Of course, the group's first friends were present at the table too, from Baku, Oki, Madame Bijoux and Scarlet.

As the feast proceeded, Elwin was approached by Styriax and asking him to walk with her for a bit. They stopped in front of the hall's huge fire place, with roaring flames.

"Elwin, you know that you and your friends have to face a very dangerous and deceitful enemy!", Elwin with a grave face but confident of his newfound internal power, that was getting stronger, was aware of the dangers that they have to face, but mostly was preoccupied for his dear friends, than for himself. In fact, was his idea to drag them to this world and in spite of that, gave him more courage to full fil this task.

"I know Styriax, and I'm ready to face it!" Good!" Stiriax replied. "I like your confidence and courage!". Styriax said to Elwin. "I want you to give this ring to Alyssa; it's called Imossam, and was forged in the deepest parts of my realm by the spirits of the dead witches of Vernus Land, killed by the Dark One, long ago!". Elwin looked at her with a growing curiosity and anticipation." This is the Ring of the Dead?" Elwin said. "Yes!", Stiriax replied, moving around him from right to left like the wind, appearing and disappearing at will.

"It is a powerful ring, infused with their energy but sometimes can be unpredictable and dangerous until it will bond with her energy, and remember that we need a bit of darkness in our lives to keep the demons away!".

"Thank you Styriax!", Elwin replied, and perplexed by the notion of 'we need a bit of darkness in our lives to keep the demons away'.

Handing him the ring and explaining that Alyssa was the only one in the group able to control the ring like Mircalla and for that matter in the entirety of the Shardana Land.

It was made in silver with a black tourmaline stone. "The stone contains part of the spirits of the witches, that she can call on them for help, when all of you, need it the most, to make you invisible and shield you from when…!", Styriax stopped and looked towards the tables; Adriana was watching and keeping an eye out on the situation.

"From when…?" Elwin replied. "You see Elwin, it will be a time when you need to meet the Dark One's most feared righthand servant!", Stiriax continued. "A necromancer of immense powers; its powers are not physical one, but spiritual and mental ones.

You and your friends have to go through, and hopefully, pass this task!".

Elwin with a grave and a bit confused face, was listening very carefully.

"You need to enter, the darkest and deepest parts of the Hellebore forest, a place of shadows, beyond the veil of Shardana!". "Adriana didn't mention this to us?" Elwin added.

"She knows that this task, is going to be very dangerous and challenging, so she asked me, for my blessings and help for the group, hence the giving of the Imossam's Ring!".

“Now, give me your hands and keep the Imossam Ring on your right hand, but without wearing it and you need to listen very carefully Elwin, because you need to speak to the group after this!”.

At the first touch Stiriax hands were solid, as all hands should be, but while she was talking, they started to become transparent and smoky, enveloping Elwin’s hands and forearms to. “Your mind must be free by any worry and fear, remember this is a test and the only weapons that you can take with you are the staffs that Mobromora have given to all of you and remember, that they still need to be named and yours armours!”.

“Adriana and I will take you to the middle of the Hellebore Forest, you will be accompanied by some of the Trolls of the Guneria village and your familiars, but only half way, then you must continue on your owns, even without your familiars!”.

Elwin then looked back toward the tables to see what his friends were doing and noticed that all of them were looking toward him with reassuring faces that made him feel safe.

“Remember, Elwin that the darkness in this pure form will try to deceive your eyes!”.

Styriax added. “Trust your instincts!”.

“So, when all of you, will reach a small clearing in the forest, a black stone Menhir will stand before you, with carving all over it, all of you must touch with your right hands, before you enter the tunnel and wear the armours that we made for you.

On your left you will see a kind of passage made by trees, it will look very dark and not very welcoming, that’s one of the many entrances to the Land of Vernus, where the dark forces reside, and the one you must take. The Trolls and your familiars will stay in the clearing next the stone Menhir, waiting for all of you to return!" Styriax continued.

"At the end of the tunnel you will see the beginning, of what we call the Black Lake, with in the sky a waning moon. It's an illusion and the lake is enchanted. Do not touch the waters, or you will wake the water creatures that dwell in the deeps of the lake.

The only lights that you will see, except for the feeble light of the waning moon, will be the torches that the trolls have given to you. You will notice that they may dim a bit and wish that they will work for all the duration of your journey.

At the shore of the lake, a young lone little girl, will appear before you, crying, looking lost and trying to get your attention. Whatever you do, do not speak to her, do not engaged with her. She's not what she appears to be. This is the Necromancer, trying to lead you astray and testing your courage and strength!"

Elwin continued to listen with a touch of fear and worry, but sure of his internal strength.

"She will try to talk to you over and over, trying to single out any of you that shows any weakness or fear. Do not look at her. You all need to circle, the entire perimeter of the lake.

She will be following you, and still trying to talk to any of you and asking, where are you going. You mustn't talk back to her or acknowledge her.

You will notice with your peripheral vision and your gut feelings, that her appearance is starting to change, getting taller and larger; do not look back; you must control your fears and remember that Alyssa will have the ring with her, and all the amulets given to all of you by your loved ones!" Styriax continued.

“By now, you are almost half-way through the lake; you will start to hear voices all around you, coming from amongst the large trees in the shores of the lake.

You’all notice a lot of silhouettes amongst the trees, whispering, dark and full of sadness. Those voices, without warning, will start to make horrible screeching sound, trying to scare all of you; you must stay focused. They will tease you and play on your deepest and darkest fears, but you mustn’t focus on them, you must focus on the task, you have no choice, if you and your friends want to come back to Zinnigha Perdaxia, you all, must finish the task!”

Elwin looking back at the table where his friends were sitting and seeing, that they’re looking back at him too, while Styriax continued to explain the task.

“Those silhouettes are the souls trapped by the Necromancer through the ages of her kin and from not only our world but probably yours too!”

Then, Elwin remembered Oscar’s story about the lost people from our world.

‘May that be, that some of those souls amongst the trees, are some of those lost people?’, he asked to himself.

“You must focus on your task and keep walking; you will have no choice, but to keep walking!” Styriax continued.

“Do not look around even if the sounds around, sound unbearable and full of hatred.

Remember, she will be still around all of you, getting larger and scarier ready to pounce at any moment. You must control your fears. The screams will be getting more and more unbearable, she’s torturing them at the same time as she’s following all of you and the more you will get nearer the end, the more she will get unpleasant.

When you are almost at the end of the length of the lake, you'll notice that your staffs will start to emanate a faint glow, and you will feel a warm feeling entering your bodies.

They're connecting with your auras and the energy field, the Iag.

This is the time that in your mind, the staffs will introduce their names to the group…!"

Disconnecting her hands from Elwin, Styriax, stepped back and sat on the first chair that was available.

In the background in a dark corner of the Great Hall, Artier was trying to listen what Styriax was saying to Elwin, but was interrupted by Madame Bijoux, sending him scouring back outside.

"When we will have to start this last task before the battle, Styriax?" Elwin asked.

"I believe that will be the day after tomorrow, in the early evening, because you need to talk and explain to your friends first, what they need to do with you!". Elwin was excited and a bit preoccupied but at the same time, looking forward to this challenge with his dear friends.

"Do not be afraid, although it's a very dangerous place to be, I have all the confidence that you and all the others will do well. Remember that you have the ring, Imossam, that the Necromancer fear!" Styriax added.

Finally, Adriana, seeing Elwin looking a bit concerned, approached them and at the same time thanking Styriax for her valuable help and knowledge.

"Why you didn't mention this final task to us earlier, Adriana?" Elwin asked her.

"I didn't want to worry all of you earlier on!" Adriana said, bowing her head.

"As I wasn't allowed to mention this until now, by the orders of the Shining Ones".

"You see Elwin, Aat wanted to keep the Iag Energy, pure and safe until now, because they want to see when you and the group, eventually, will meet the Necromancer in the Vernus Land, what would be the response on the group Energy field, around such evil!", Adriana added.

"I see!" Elwin replied. "So the Shining Ones will be there too with us?", Elwin added.

"They're always around, even if we don't see them!", Adriana said.

"Now, tomorrow you will spend the morning in the company of your friends and you can explain, more in detail what Styriax told you to the others!", Adriana added.

With a mystified, worried and at the same time with a dash of excitement, Elwin accepted the new task.

The feast was almost finished, and everyone was starting to proceed towards the exit.

Prince Mordrek went towards Aqua, asking her how she's enjoying this new and unusual experience in the world of Zinnigha Perdaxia. Looking at him straight in the eyes and saying that this was the best thing that could have happened to her. He liked Aqua's straight forward and confident attitude and his feelings were starting to make him a bit wobbly. They walked for a short while towards the Palace's gardens and Mordrek took Aqua hand and kissed her goodbye.

The group were astounded by this site and happy for Aqua, then she replied to them to come down, because there wasn't nothing to worry about.

Everyone, after the feast, thanked the King and Adriana for the constructive evening and left for their respective homes.

The group by now, very tired and sleepy, headed towards the circular room to rest for the night.

Alyssa asked Elwin. “What was all of that about with Styriax?” with the rest of the group, looking at him.

“I’all let you know tomorrow guys, for now please get some rest!”. He replied to them.

Clutching the Ring of the Dead and putting it inside one his pockets, closed his eyes, and went to sleep.

Chapter Thirteen

'The Necromancer'

The group headed outside into the Palace gardens after their breakfast. The weather was pleasantly warm, and the sun was shining bright, but the group didn't feel the warmth, as they're picking up some tension and worries from Elwin.

Walking at the end of the path, they found an old circular temple. "Looks like a Folly from our world!" Oscar said. "Yes, it does!" Lunette replied.

"Who do you think is the person portrayed in the middle?" Alyssa pointing out the statue there. The base of the pedestal in which the statue of a woman was standing, was inscribed with some sort of language that none of them could read.

"Let's no worry about it, at the moment, we need to talk!" Elwin said. "Yes, we're all ears!"

Oscar replied.

The group sat on the circular benches around the perimeter of the temple.

"First of all, I need to give this to you, Alyssa!" Elwin said. Taking the ring out of his pocket and hand it to her.

"What is it?" Lunette said. "A ring!" Alyssa replied. "That looks beautiful!" Aqua added.

"This is the Ring of the Dead, given to me by Styriax last night, to pass to you Alyssa!".

Elwin added.

Everyone in astonishment, was looking at Alyssa, and the ring. "Put it on!" Aqua said.

Alyssa, very pleased by this unexpected gift, asked Elwin which hand she should use to put the ring on.

"The right hand, I guess!" Elwin replied.

As Alyssa was putting the ring on the finger, her green eyes became shining like emeralds and from the ring, a light darkish smoke was emanating from the Tourmaline stone, enveloping the entire Temple and the group in it, growing larger, obscuring the brightness of that beautiful bright morning. From the dark smoke, some silhouettes came out and started flying around them, only to come to a standstill in front of them.

The group were amazed by what was happening before their eyes, with Alyssa telling them not to be afraid, "These are the spirits of the dead witches, checking on me." With feeble, overleaping, echoing voices, they welcome Alyssa as the new keeper but not all of them were happy about it and they voiced that to her.

"Where is Mircalla?" some asked to Alyssa in a patronising and arrogant voice. Before Alyssa could say anything, Elwin with a firm voice stated to them. "This Ring has being given to Alyssa by the Wise Mother of the shadow fairies, Styriax!".

Making screeches of disappointment, some of them disappeared back into the Ring but mostly were happy to help them at the moment and to serve Alyssa, as the new bearer.

After that, the brightness of the morning came back, and everyone was astounded by Alyssa and Elwin courage. "You must keep this Ring always on your finger, Alyssa!", Elwin added, "It will help us greatly on this final task that we need to take, this early evening!", Elwin continued.

“What other task?”, Oscar asked. Elwin recounted all what Styriax mentioned to him the day before, and after a very long explanation, many questions were raised to Elwin.

From, “how could we do this?” To “what if we fail the task?”

But the excitement was too intense to control and amazingly, after the early tension, all of them were feeling stronger and confident.

Heading back to the castle, playing around with each other, Adriana was waiting for them on top the staircase and welcoming them back to the castle.

“Please, is there anything that you would like to ask me about the task?” Adriana said to the group, looking at their faces.

Most of them were happy and clear by Elwin’s explanation. Only Alyssa asked Adriana.

“Why Styriax, choose me, as the bearer of the Ring of the Dead?” “ You see Alyssa, you are the only one in the group that could summon the dead witches and ask them to work for you, for the group protection and the benefit of Zinnigha Perdaxa!”

“The other one is, of course Mircalla!” Alyssa then said.

“Some of them weren’t happy for me to have the ring!”

“Don’t worry, when in the presence of the Necromancer, they will unleash all their power against her!”. Adriana added. “Her?”, Elwin asked. “So, she a female then!” Lunette, added. “This it’s what we think here in Zinnigha Perdaxa!”.

Everyone was listening to Adriana and waiting for more information about the Necromancer. “She was the beautiful Elf Priestess of the Black Lake and the surrounding forests long ago, but she had a dark hearth and with her black arts, enslaved all the creatures that lived there, including some of her own kin that didn't leave, and using them to make offering to the Dark One; yes, she was the first Elf to worship and swear allegiance to him. She's thousands of years old!".

"Where all the other elves went, after escaping the Necromancer?", Aqua said.

"They've founded another city in the Northern Lands at the slopes of the tallest peak on the Gennargentu mountain's, called Aureum, the Golden City!". Adriana added.

Oscar, then mentions. "Is where Tiddraigh sister's lives?".

"Yes, good memory Oscar; Fera and other dragons reside in the North and have good relations with the elves of the Golden City!". Adriana said and adding. "It's a beautiful city to the Dark One's infection, that's gripping the land of Shardana."

"Do you remember the day of your familiars introduction? The flying creatures that the Evil Five were riding as harpies?" She added.

All of them nodding yes. "Those are some of the elves that the Necromancer manage to corrupt for her advantage and unable to reverse back into the light!", "So who are the Evil Five then?" Oscar asked. "Are not corrupted Elves to?" Aqua added.

"No, they're actually corrupted Ladies of Simieri, Aeldry is the leader of the coven, with Ieldren, Gymerreth, Frirril and Freiri. But I still believe that few of them, in the right circumstances could be helped back to the light!". Adriana added and looking in particular at Aqua. "Now, let's get inside, because the King would like to speak with all of you!"

Adriana said.

While the group was walking towards the Great Hall, Una and Ella approached them and without saying anything, they started to fly around them and with their wands were sprinkling a sort of shining lights all over their bodies.

Adriana stopped and moved a bit back toward the wall, watching with amazement at that beautiful sight, that attracted more curious watchers, like Scarlet, Madame Bijoux and other from the royal household.

After few minutes Una and Ella left giggling and very excited. "Whoa, that's amazing what just happened!" Lunette said.

"Your'e very lucky indeed!" Adriana said, "Not everyone is that fortunate to have an extra blessing from the Blue fairies!", Adriana said.

"The Blue fairies possessed an aura of incredible power that last a life time, so even when you decide to leave our world for yours back home, their protection will be there always!", Madame Bijoux added.

The group were so happy to hear that; "An extra protection, is always welcome in any situation!" Oscar said, "we will thank them, when we come back!", Alyssa said.

After speaking to the King, and having his blessings for the task ahead, the group went to theirs rooms to prepare for the evening. The afternoon went very fast, and the group were ready to get to the forest.

Armours wore and staffs at the ready, they started to make their way back out, into the front of the castle.

While walking, Elwin reminded the group; "have you named your staff's yet?"

They all nodded yes. "Remember to keep those names to yourselves guys!".

"Sure, don't worry Elwin, will do!" Alyssa replied.

Outside, all the familiars were waiting for them with the Guneria Trolls too. At the top of the castle in one of the balconies, the King and Princess Marygolda were waving goodbye, with all the royal household all over the staircase, also waiving and sending all the best wishes to them for a fast and safe return.

So, they went marching with pride, surrounded by the familiars, Adriana and about eight huge Guneria Trolls, grunting all the way.

After about an hour, they finally reached the clearing in the forest where the black stone Menhir was situated, in which they gather around it and one at the time, running their hands in a circular motion against the stone.

To the left, there it was, the tunnel that Styriax mentioned, looking forbidding and darker than they expected.

"Right, you're ready to enter?" Adriana said. "Yes, we are!", they all said at the same time, holding hands and looking at each other, then Oscar added, "Definitely, this is going to be a bit different, than to be at school, guys!".

All of them cracked a laugh. So, they said goodbye to all and went through the tunnel, looking back at Adriana and smiling back at her.

The passage was getting darker at every step, until after a short while, they came through the end of the tunnel and before them, there it was the Black Lake.

The group were standing together and starting to light the torches. "Be on your guard guys!" Elwin said.

Looking around, they notice that this place, not only was darker than your usual forest, but the atmosphere, definitely was sinister and silent. No sound at all, only their own footsteps.

So, they began to walk on the right side of the lake with Elwin at the front, followed by Alyssa, Lunette, Aqua and Oscar, who was looking over his shoulders.

They came across a bend in the perimeter of the lake and there she was, a little girl, wearing a long dirty white dress, crying and holding her hands in the face.

The group froze. "Do not look at her!" Elwin, said to the group. "Keep walking guys!"

Alyssa added.

Everyone, holding their staff very tight, continuing walking, trying to ignore her.

"Can you help me, please?" she said to them, in a begging voice. "Do not answer!"

Elwin said.

The walk was a bit difficult not only because the dim light but also for the tree roots, that were sticking up everywhere from the ground.

"Why are you not answering me?" She spoke. The group unmoved, kept walking. On their right side they saw the large trees that Styriax mentioned, and they looked even more ominous than when she explained.

Still, the little girl was following them, but not getting too close. Suddenly, Aqua said, "Look! The shadows amongst the tree are moving!". "Yes, I can see them too!", Lunette added.

They could hear them whispering and making a low screeching sound, trying to get nearer them, but something was stopping them.

They couldn't step out of the tree line, as if they were bound to it and in the moon light, they gleamed faintly, horribly and a yell of the most piercing animalistic intensity roared all around them. The group were still walking in terror, when Oscar missed a step and his left foot, slipped into the water, carrying with it some stones and making a muffled sound that rippled around the lake.

Everyone stopped and looked at him, with Elwin gesturing at the group, not to get too close to the shores of the lake; he hadn't almost finished his sentence, that a dark slithering form, was approaching them from the middle of the lake.

"Step back guys, quick!" Elwin said, in a worried voice. From the lake, there it was a familiar creature to the group; the huge black snake, that attached them when they were on the way to the Guneria village to meet Orcu.

The snake approached them with speed and halfway of the water, he raised his huge body out of the water. On the left side of the snake's body, you could see the remains of Bolzac's arrow, still embedded on it.

"I can't believe it!" Oscar shouted. "Gather around and don't show any fear!" Elwin added.

The snake came out of the water completely, looking even larger than they remembered, launching itself toward the group, that with their staffs at the ready and calling in their minds, the names to come and help them to stop this abomination. Oscar taking the situation as an almost personal level, went a bit forward towards the snake and from his staff, a blindingly light came out of it, making the snake to stop on his track, stepping back and again, launching toward Oscar with an angry hiss. The light emanating from Oscar's staff, was creating a bubble of protection, not only on him, but all over the group.

In the midst of all what was happening, the little girl was starting to change and was not looking any more like a sweet lost little girl; her appearance was getting more scary, larger and darker.

Alyssa, Aqua and Lunette, noticed the change and both of them turned back facing it and with theirs staffs at the ready for what was coming. Alyssa also was wondering if this was the time to start to use the Ring of the Dead, but something was stopping her. "Not yet!" she mumbled to herself.

The screams from the forest's shadows were getting, louder and more uncomfortable.

The air was heavy. Elwin approached Oscar on his right-hand side and together with their staff were focusing their energy against the snake and a double beam of light came out from them, so strong and bright, that all around for a moment, looked like midday.

The two combine energies sliced the snake in two, killing it instantly, and as it was felling down, the ground around them trembled. "We done it, Elwin!" exclaimed Oscar with a shaking voice and hugging him. The light around them was dimming and every one attention was towards the little girl in which she now appeared as her true form, the Necromancer. A revolting old hag, a mixture of a dwarf and a goblin-like figure, that at this moment was very angry and surprised that a group of young humans managed to kill a very dangerous creature from the dark side.

"Gather together!" Elwin shouted to the group. In the meantime, while the dark shadows were still screaming all around, in pain and despair and there in a clearing between the shores of the lake and the forest, were standing Elwin and his friends, face to face with the Necromancer...

To be continued.

Biography

Born in the beautiful island of Sardinia in 1969, isn't the only bookworm of the family, as his mother - Cordeddu Giorgina – is already an accomplished writer in Italy.

Studied Fine Art in Cagliari and Graphic Design in London. A painter and sculptor of Dark Art and self-proclaimed Bio-Mechanical Artist with one of his works being shortlisted at the Summer Exhibition in the Royal Academy of Arts in London in 2008. Also other of his works being published in other books, like on "Planet Earth" in 2009.

HIs passion for fantasy and horror fiction, has been a safe heaven, throughout his life, from a young age, till now, imagining and creating a magical realm to escape the, sometimes, cruel daily life.

A lot of his inspirations are born thru his dreams and the interaction with the people around, that he did immortalise in the form of drawings and sculptures.

This is his first story and that came when he was in his thoughts walking around the wilderness in the beloved Sardinia, an ancient island full of mythology and folklore, with a dash of Northern European folklore from the beautiful Scotland where he resides at the moment, in the mix.

Table of Contents

europe books